TALES OF

by G. MaTov

translated by
Shaindel Weinbach

illustrated by
Miriam Bardugo

TZADDIKIM

A wonderful collection of stories from our Sages
and the great Torah and Chassidic leaders,
arranged according to the Sidra of the week.

Published by

Mesorah Publications, ltd

in conjunction with

HAMESORAH /
Jerusalem

FIRST EDITION
First Impression . . . October 1987
SECOND EDITION
First Impression . . . January 1999

Published and Distributed by
MESORAH PUBLICATIONS, Ltd.
Brooklyn, New York 11223
in conjunction with
HAMESORAH / Jerusalem

Distributed in Israel by
MESORAH MAFITZIM / J. GROSSMAN
Rechov Harav Uziel 117
Jerusalem, Israel

Distributed in Europe by
J. LEHMANN HEBREW BOOKSELLERS
20 Cambridge Terrace
Gateshead, Tyne and Wear
England NE8 1RP

THE ARTSCROLL YOUTH SERIES ·
TALES OF TZADDIKIM / VOL. I — BEREISHIS
© Copyright 1987 by MESORAH PUBLICATIONS, Ltd.
1969 Coney Island Avenue / Brooklyn, N.Y. 11223 / (718) 339-1700

ISBN:
0-89906-825-1 (hard cover)

Printed in the United States of America by Noble Book Press Corp.
Bound by Sefercraft Quality Bookbinders, Ltd., Brooklyn, N.Y.

Table of Contents

Parashas Vayeira

Parashas Chayei Sarah

৽ Parashas Toldos

৽ Parashas Vayeitzei

৽ Parashas Vayishlach

৽ Parashas Vayeishev

TALES OF
TZADDIKIM

פָּרָשַׁת בְּרֵאשִׁית

Parashas Bereishis

The World Bears Witness

בְּרֵאשִׁית בָּרָא אֱ-לֹהִים אֵת הַשָּׁמַיִם וְאֵת הָאָרֶץ

In the beginning G-d created the heavens and the earth (1:1)

R' Yehudah Halevi, the great Jewish poet of the Golden Age of Spain, had a gentile neighbor who was also a poet. But this gentile denied the existence of a Creator. He insisted that the world had come into being all by itself. The two men held many discussions but the Jew could not convince the gentile of the foolishness of his philosophy.

One day this gentile poet composed a beautiful piece of poetry but could not complete the final lines; his inspiration had left him. He got up to take a stroll in his garden and refresh his mind.

Just then, R' Yehudah Halevi passed by the house and could not help seeing the sheet of paper lying on the desk right by the open window. He leaned over and began reading the unfinished poem. Then and there, R' Yehudah Halevi added a stanza that put a perfect finishing touch to the poem.

When the gentile poet returned from his walk, he went back to his desk. There was his masterpiece, completed to perfection! He could hardly believe his eyes! He knew that he had not written those beautiful lines. Who had? Full of wonder, he ran over to his neighbor and told him about the strange incident.

"Why are you so surprised?" R' Yehudah said coolly. "The poem wrote itself!"

"You know that such a thing is impossible!" the gentile said seriously. "Don't joke. A work of art does not come into being by itself!"

"Aha!" said R' Yehudah exultantly. "You admit this freely. A poem does not write itself. Very well, but neither does such a magnificent world as the one we live in, equipped with such intricate workings, create itself!"

The gentile finally admitted defeat. To be sure, the world had to have been created by some exalted Being.

In the Lions' Den

וּרְדוּ בִּדְגַת הַיָּם וּבְעוֹף הַשָּׁמַיִם וּבְכָל חַיָּה הָרֹמֶשֶׂת עַל הָאָרֶץ

And rule over the fish of the sea and the birds of the heavens and over all the beasts which crawl upon the earth (1:28)

R' Chaim ben Attar, who wrote the *Or Hachaim* commentary on the Torah, is one of the few great men of Jewish history called *kadosh* — holy. He is popularly referred to as the *Or Hachaim Hakadosh*.

He did not want to earn his livelihood by using his knowledge of Torah and therefore as a youth he learned a trade; he became a jeweler.

When he had learned his trade well, he found work with a gentile silversmith. R' Chaim did not work regular hours. Whenever he needed money, which was not often, he would take on a piece of work and complete it as best and as quickly as he knew how.

The gentile did not especially love Jews but he did respect R' Chaim's skill. He needed such a good worker. Besides, R' Chaim was dependable, reliable and never complained. At first he tried paying R' Chaim high wages but he saw that R' Chaim kept away for longer stretches at a time. He then lowered his wages but still R' Chaim refused to work more than a bare minimum.

The jeweler acquired a reputation as a very skilled craftsman. His pieces of jewelry were works of art, the richest people where his customers. Small wonder that when the Sultan was planning his daughter's wedding, he summoned the jeweler to the palace and gave him a long list of the things he required. He insisted that all must be ready at the appointed time! Woe to the jeweler if he failed to satisfy his royal customer!

The jeweler glowed with pleasure and pride at having been entrusted with such an important order. What a privilege to be the Sultan's jeweler. From now on, he would never lack customers!

The jeweler worked diligently but when the appointed date arrived he saw to his horror that he had not completed the order. The Sultan was furious. No one disappointed the ruler and lived! It was the greatest privilege in the land to be able to serve the Sultan. There was no excuse for not having filled the order within the specified time.

"I want that man killed at once. Throw him into the lions' den," roared the enraged ruler.

"But I am not to blame, Your Majesty," the jeweler said, bowing low. "It is all the fault of my Jewish worker. He was to see that the work was completed. He deserves to be killed, not I. He is a lazy, good-for-nothing who hardly set foot in the shop. It is because of him that Your Majesty's order is not ready on time."

"Very well," said the Sultan. "You are excused but your assistant will be thrown to the lions."

The Sultan's palace was surrounded by beautiful, well-kept grounds that stretched for acres and acres and were walled in by a high stone fence. In the midst of this garden was a lions' den. Now and then the Sultan would punish some rebellious servant by casting him to the lions. The lions would be starved so as to be thoroughly hungry for their prey. There would be one long, blood-curdling shriek as the victim was torn to pieces, and then quiet, as the animals fed hungrily upon their victim. The roaring of the hungry lions alone put the Sultan's fear into the hearts of his servants.

The Sultan gave the order. His soldiers hurried to R' Chaim's home, surrounded it and seized him. They expected him to protest his innocence, to weep and scream. But all he asked was that he be allowed to take some books and his *tallis* and *tefillin*.

"Ha!" they laughed. "Do you think that you are going on a vacation? On a pleasure trip? Will you teach the animals to read and write? You will not last long enough to open up one of your precious books! Well, it makes no difference to us."

"What a joke," they thought, but waited the few

minutes that it took R' Chaim to gather up his things.

News of this terrible sentence flew through the Jewish community. It was a day of mourning. All shops were closed. The Jews left their homes and went to R' Chaim's home to accompany him on his last walk. Not an eye was dry. People walked as if it were a funeral.

The group proceeded slowly towards the Sultan's palace. All around swarmed the city's Arab residents. They wore smug, happy expressions on their faces for they despised this clever race and were happy to see its most revered leader being led to his death.

R' Chaim strode calmly between the soldiers. They did not need to hold or restrain him. He walked confidently, gazing straight ahead. When they reached the palace gates, he turned to the crying Jews and comforted them, "There is no need to weep. The A-mighty will save me from the jaws of the wild beasts. I place my trust in Him."

The guards led R' Chaim through the immaculate gardens, the clipped hedges, towering trees, fragrant bushes and blooming flower beds until they came to the high wall that surrounded the lions' den. R' Chaim was given over to the custody of the lion keepers. They were adept at their job. They tied a rope around his waist and lowered R' Chaim, over the wall and into the lions' den. Then they stood back and waited for the pitiful shriek that would rend the air. But all was quiet. Strangely, eerily quiet. They could not even hear the usual sounds that the pack of lions made as they paced back and forth. A minute passed, another minute. All was still. What was going on down there?!

The guards could not believe their ears. Overcome by curiosity, they leaned over the top of the pit and looked down. They could not believe their eyes!

Something very strange and wonderful indeed! The animals had always pounced upon their victim even before he touched the ground. This time they had not done anything. They stood very still, watching R' Chaim.

"The animals are probably not hungry," said one of them. "After all, this has come without any notice. The animals were fed as usual yesterday evening. We have not had any time to starve them."

The guards went around on tiptoe all day, waiting for the single shriek that would signal the death of the man inside the pit. But there was no sound, not even the usual scurrying and scuffling of animals. It was uncanny!

Three days and three nights passed. The guards were sure that by now the lions had devoured their victim even if he had not cried out. And now it was time to feed them again.

The guards looked over the high wall, expecting to see scattered human bones. To their amazement, the Jewish rabbi was well, even happy. There he sat, wrapped in his *tallis* and crowned by his *tefillin*; there was an unearthly look on his face, like that of an angel. The biggest surprise of all was the lions. They crouched at his feet like so many pet dogs, basking in the sun as if after a full meal. They even seemed to be listening to the sound of his sweet voice.

The guards rubbed their eyes to see if they were not mistaken, if they were not seeing some strange mirage. Some of them ran to the palace to tell the Sultan about the incredible sight.

"I don't believe it!" the Sultan said. "I must see this for myself!" He followed the guards to the lions' den. He stood on tiptoe and peeked over the stone wall. It was

just as they had said! There was the Jewish rabbi, sitting peacefully, without a care in the world! At first the Sultan was dumbstruck. Then he ordered the game-keepers to lower down a rope and pull the rabbi out of the pit.

When R' Chaim stood before him, truly unharmed, the Sultan fell to his feet, begging, "Forgive me! Forgive me! You are a holy man, a saint! Please do not punish me!"

The Sultan led R' Chaim back to the palace. There, in front of all his ministers, he announced, "From now on, my palace doors will always be open to you. You must become my chief advisor for no one is as wise and holy as you!"

That day became a holiday for the Jews of Morocco. They celebrate it, year after year, as the day upon which R' Chaim was saved from the jaws of the wild beasts.

Beasts or Innocent Lambs?

וּרְדוּ בִּדְגַת הַיָּם וּבְעוֹף הַשָּׁמַיִם וּבְכָל חַיָּה הָרֹמֶשֶׂת עַל הָאָרֶץ

And rule over the fish of the sea and the birds of the heavens and over all the beasts which crawl upon the earth (1:28)

Eretz Yisrael is more dependent on rain than other countries for it does not have many rivers or lakes. If little rain falls during the winter, which is the rainy season, there are hard times ahead.

One year, very little rain fell. The ground was parched and nothing grew. There were no crops and no food. What little food still remained was very expensive; the poor were on the verge of starvation.

The Torah scholars of Jerusalem, who lived upon the meager handout which they received from the *yeshivos*, suffered most, for they could not afford to buy food at high prices. The people who had supported the *yeshivos* in better times could no longer afford to give money. Everyone suffered, but the Torah community was hardest hit.

As always, in times of stress and suffering, the rabbis and leaders of Jerusalem gathered to discuss the problem. They decided to send a rabbi abroad to raise money from Jewish communities across the sea. Surely the good people there would not refuse to help.

No one really wanted the task. It was very difficult to leave home and travel to a strange place, even harder to describe the difficult plight and ask for funds. How much more pleasant to remain at home and immerse oneself in the refreshing sea of Talmud!

Lots were drawn and the task fell to R' Avraham Galanti. His vast knowledge and piety were well known, for he had spent his whole life totally devoted to Torah. He did not know his way around in foreign lands. But R' Avraham was not one to complain. He knew how desperate the situation was; someone had to do something, and it might just as well be he. Packing a small satchel of belongings, he set out for the port of Jaffa where a ship would take him across the sea to Turkey, to the Jewish community of Constantinople.

The sea voyage itself took several weeks but finally the captain sighted land from the lookout deck. He noticed something very strange. There were no sailors loading and unloading ships with wares from all over the world. Instead there were people running back and forth, as if panic-stricken. People had gathered on rooftops and were gesturing frantically. Armed soldiers patrolled the deserted streets.

The captain was frightened. He would not dock. He did not want to expose his passengers or crew to an epidemic or any other dangerous situation. He had other ports to visit. He did not have to stop at Constantinople.

R' Avraham Galanti was upset. Constantinople was his main destination. He had been counting upon its Jewish community, which had always been known for the generosity of its members. He had explicit instructions from the great men of Jerusalem. He must find a way to carry out those instructions.

R' Avraham went to the captain and explained his dilemma, begging only for a small rowboat to land him on shore. The sailor need not step foot on shore; he could row right back to ship.

The captain was very reluctant. He did not want to contaminate his entire ship with some unknown disease. He tried to dissuade R' Avraham from his dangerous plan, but, finally, seeing that he was determined to get to shore, the captain agreed. He could not help but be impressed by the Jew's dignity and saintliness.

The small boat was lowered from the deck. R' Avraham and a sailor descended into it. As soon as they neared land, R' Avraham disembarked hastily and went ashore while the sailor sped back to ship.

R' Avraham had barely put his foot on dry land when two soldiers rushed to his side. "If you value your life, you would be wise to call back that sailor and have him take you away from here!" they warned.

"Why?" R' Avraham wanted to know.

"Two fierce lions have escaped from the Sultan's private zoo. They are loose in town and have created a reign of terror. No one dares leave his home. Everyone is watching from the rooftops, where it is safest. We are doing our best to catch them but no one dares approach the beasts, and the Sultan wants them back alive."

Just at that moment, there was a blood-curdling roar. The soldiers panicked and ran. R' Avraham was left alone, standing motionless.

A lion bounded forward, all of its senses alert. It had not eaten for several days and was ravenous. But as soon as it reached R' Avraham, it crouched down docilely, like a tame dog. People on the nearby rooftops closed their eyes; they were afraid to look. They were certain that the man had no chance of survival. But when they realized that a miracle was taking place, they leaned over, the better to watch the strange sight.

R' Avraham was leading the lion by its mane, and the lion was following like an obedient pet. On their way to the Sultan's palace, they came across the second lion. This lion was hurling its huge body against a door, trying to break it down and force its way in. R' Avraham called to it softly. The beast turned its head and looked at him. Suddenly its body relaxed and it pattered up to R' Avraham and looked meekly up into his eyes. It allowed the rabbi to grasp its mane, too, and the group went on, R' Avraham flanked by two tame lions.

The streets were utterly deserted. Not a sound could be heard. People on the roofs gazed and gaped; they could not believe their own eyes. Here was a Jewish rabbi, walking along, fearlessly, leading two dangerous beasts, much bigger than he, as if they were timid sheep!

The strange procession soon reached the Sultan's private zoo. R' Avraham walked over to the two open cages and led the lions in. They made no protest whatsoever. After they were inside, he closed the gate securely and locked it with an extra bar. The lions were safely imprisoned.

As R' Avraham was walking away he met the Sultan and his ministers who had now finally dared to go outside. The Sultan begged R' Avraham to come with him to the palace. He wished to speak to him and thank him for his courageous act.

R' Avraham was placed at the Sultan's side. The Sultan asked him who he was and how he had dared approach the lions. He wanted to know what miraculous power he had exerted over them.

R' Avraham explained that he was from Jerusalem and that he had come to raise money for the famine-stricken Jewish community.

The Sultan smiled. "And I thought that you were a professional lion tamer! Or a magician. But if you are not, what gave you the courage to approach those famished beasts?"

R' Avraham bowed before the Sultan and said, "You can see, Your Majesty, that I am but a weak, old man. I have never been known for my strength. Nor am I a magician, for the black arts are forbidden by our Torah. You ask how I succeeded in asserting my will over these wild beasts. Let me explain: our Sages have taught that a brave man is one who can conquer his own evil nature. All my life I have fought against my wicked impulses. I have sought to purify myself and have succeeded to the extent that I am not afraid of anything — except for the

A-mighty, of course!

"Another thing, Your Majesty. When *Hashem* created the beasts of the earth, he instilled in them a natural fear of man. This fear, however, is present only when a man behaves like a man and not like a beast. When a man corrupts his nature, he spoils his G-dly image. Small wonder, then, that instead of the animal being afraid of him, he is afraid of the animal!"

These words, so full of natural wisdom, deeply impressed the Sultan and his ministers. The Sultan instinctively felt that here was a very holy man who truly bore the image of G-d and did great credit to it. Here was a man graced by divine spirit. He felt humbled and awed.

"I am grateful to you for having saved us from the terror of the escaped lions. I wish to reward you generously and to help your worthy cause," he said and instructed his servants to take R' Avraham to his treasure vaults and give him a huge reward.

Having successfully fulfilled his mission, R' Avraham left Constantinople to return to Jerusalem. The Sultan and his court accompanied R' Avraham to his ship and sent him off with their warmest thanks and good wishes.

Everything Is For the Best

וַיַּרְא אֱ-לֹהִים אֶת כָּל אֲשֶׁר עָשָׂה וְהִנֵּה טוֹב

"And Hashem saw all that He had done and it was good" (1:31)

Once R' Akiva went upon a long journey, taking with him three things: a donkey, a rooster and a candle.

The donkey he took to ride upon and to carry his bundles. He took the rooster to wake him up at the crack of dawn. The candle was to give him light so that he could study Torah at night.

R' Akiva rode and rode until evening fell. He entered a town and went looking for an inn to spend the night but this town had no inn.

Knocking at the door of one house, he asked, "Do you have room to take in a lodger for the night?"

"No!" the people answered abruptly. "Move on!"

R' Akiva tried one house after another, but no one agreed to let him stay for the night. He stood in the middle of town, wondering what to do. It was dark and chilly. Where would he spend the night? R' Akiva did not despair. He said to himself, "Everything that *Hashem* does — is for the best!"

He did not wish to remain in a town whose inhabitants were such wicked, inhospitable people. He decided to sleep outdoors in a nearby field.

R' Akiva settled down under a tree, lit his candle, fed his donkey and rooster — and then sank deep into studying Torah. He was so engrossed that he forgot where he was — out in the open, all alone, in the middle of the night.

Suddenly, a mighty roar pierced the stillness of the night. R' Akiva saw a huge lion pouncing upon his donkey. Another minute — and the donkey was no more. The lion had killed it.

He had not recovered from the terrible shock when a wild cat leaped upon his rooster from a different direction. R' Akiva was about to go to save it when a blast of wind blew his candle out.

R' Akiva stood in the dark. Now he was truly helpless.

He no longer had his donkey, his rooster or his candle. But he was not discouraged. In fact, he said, "Everything that *Hashem* does — is for the best."

He was still standing there, puzzling over the events, when he saw a light from afar. Fire! The town where he had almost spent the night was on fire! Its wooden houses with their thatched roofs would be destroyed in minutes!

Soon, R' Akiva heard voices. A band of robbers had attacked the town that night, captured all of its inhabitants and set their homes on fire. They were now leading their prisoners through the field. Due to the darkness, they did not discern R' Akiva standing by the tree.

Suddenly, he understood everything: why the lion had devoured the donkey, why the wild cat had killed his rooster, and why the wind had blown out his candle. Had the donkey brayed or the rooster crowed in fear, the thieves would have heard them. Had they seen the candle, they would have captured R' Akiva as well.

Indeed, everything had turned out for the best!

R' Akiva thanked *Hashem* for having saved him and he continued on his way.

(Tractate *Berachos* 60b)

The Spider and the Wasp

וַיַּרְא אֱ־לֹהִים אֶת כָּל אֲשֶׁר עָשָׂה וְהִנֵּה טוֹב

And G-d saw all that He had done and behold, it was good (1:31)

One day, before he ruled over Israel, David sat in his garden, watching a wasp devour a spider.

"Master of the world!" he said with wonder, "what

purpose do these two creatures serve? The wasp does not make honey; it steals it from the bee. True, the spider weaves intricate cobwebs, but of what use are these to man? We cannot make cloth from them!"

Hashem replied, "David, do you dare mock My creations? Do you dare question My wisdom? Wait and see! The time will yet come when these two creatures will serve you and you will be grateful for their existence!"

And so it came to pass.

Once, when David fled from the wrath of King Shaul, he found shelter in a cave. The king, hot on his trail, reached the spot. A large spider web covered the mouth of the cave. "Surely no one has been in there recently," he thought, "for he would have ripped apart this spider web. I will search further."

Thus, David was saved with the help of a spider.

Another time David saw the king encamped with his armies; he decided to go and steal Shaul's canteen. David wished to show the king that he bore him no ill feelings, that even when he had had the chance to kill him he had left him unharmed. When everyone was fast asleep, David slipped into the camp. Stealthily, he went to the king's tent. Avner ben Ner, the king's general, a giant of a man, was sleeping in the entrance. Avner's feet were spread wide apart and David had no difficulty reaching over and snatching the king's canteen. Suddenly, Avner moved his legs, imprisoning David between them with a grip of iron. He panicked. If the king found him here, he would surely kill him! He prayed to *Hashem* and just then a wasp flew into the tent and stung Avner on the leg. Avner did not wake up; he moved his feet, and David was free. David ran for his life. He had been saved by a wasp.

When he was safe once more, David prayed to *Hashem*, saying, "Master of the world! Who shall compare with Your deeds and Your might! All of them are praiseworthy!"

(According to Otzar Hamidrashim 77)

The Real Proof

בְּיוֹם עֲשׂוֹת ה' אֱ-לֹהִים אֶרֶץ וְשָׁמָיִם

On the day that Hashem Elokim made the earth and heaven (2:4)

A gentile once came to R' Akiva and asked, "Who created the world?"

R' Akiva replied, "*Hakadosh Baruch Hu!*"

"Prove it!" demanded the gentile.

"Come to me tomorrow and I will give you proof," said R' Akiva.

On the following day when the gentile arrived, R' Akiva asked, "What are you wearing?"

"A suit of clothing!" was the reply.

"Who made it?"

"A tailor!"

R' Akiva shook his head. "I don't believe you! Prove it!"

The gentile grew angry. "What proof do you need? Don't you know that only a tailor could have made this garment?!"

"And don't you know," R' Akiva answered him with a question as well, "that only G-d could have — and did create the world?!"

The gentile turned and left.

R' Akiva's *talmidim* then turned to their teacher and asked, "Tell us, what is the real proof?"

He said, "Dear students, just as a house testifies to the builder who constructed it and the garment to the tailor who sewed it and the door to the carpenter who made it — so does the world testify and announce to all that only *Hakadosh Baruch Hu* created it!"

When Everyone is Happy

כִּי לֹא הִמְטִיר ה' אֱ-לֹהִים עַל הָאָרֶץ

For Hashem Elokim had not caused it to rain on the earth
(2:5)

A gentile once came to R' Yehoshua ben Korcha and said, "We are good friends, are we not? I would like to rejoice together with you one day. But this opportunity never arises. For all through the year there is not one day when both Jews and gentiles celebrate. Usually when one of us is happy, the other mourns."

R' Yehoshua replied, "Oh, but there *is* one day when everyone in the world rejoices, Jews and gentiles alike! That is on the day that rain falls. And why is that so? Because without rain the world cannot continue to exist. It follows that rain brings blessing and prosperity to all and the falling of rain promotes a feeling of brotherly love and friendship among mankind. When it rains, there is much less unfounded hatred, *sinas chinam*. On the other hand, when there is drought, there is famine and suffering and everyone is unhappy. Then there is much quarreling and strife.

"It is no wonder, therefore," concluded R' Yehoshua, "that on the day that rain falls — everyone rejoices!"

(According to *Midrash Rabba Bereishis 13:4*)

A Successful Argument

לַפֶּתַח חַטָּאת רֹבֵץ

Sin crouches by the threshold (4:7)

This is the 'yetzer hara', which rules over a person from the time of his birth, not like the 'yetzer tov', which only joins a person upon his 'bar mitzvah'

(Sanhedrin 91b, and Midrash Rabba Koheles 84)

From early childhood on, Yisrael, who was to become the famous R' Yisrael of Ruzhin, showed exceptional traits and talents. At his *bar mitzvah* celebration, he was asked by one of the guests, "Tell me, Yisrael, if your *yetzer hatov* has only come to your aid today, now that you are obligated to fulfill *mitzvos*, how were you able to fight off your *yetzer hara* all these years singlehandedly?"

"Whenever he came to tempt me with any sin, I would put him off with a winning argument."

"And what was that?" the man asked, full of curiosity.

"I used to tell him that the *halachah* requires a judge to consider a case only when the two sides are present. If he wished me to consider his temptations, he must wait for the *yetzer hatov* to come on the scene and present his side of the story!"

The Leaf's Ego

כֹּל הַנִּקְרָא בִשְׁמִי וְלִכְבוֹדִי בְּרָאתִיו יְצַרְתִּיו אַף עֲשִׂיתִיו

Everyone that is called by My name, and whom I have
created for My glory, I have formed him, I have made him
(Haftorah Parashas Bereishis, Yeshayahu 43)

It was summertime. A time for relaxation, for restoring one's strength. R' Shalom Dov of Lubavitch was spending some time with his son, R' Yosef Yitzchak, in the pleasant, invigorating climate of a village. The two used to take long walks through the countryside, marveling at the beauty of *Hashem*'s world.

The fields were ripe with their golden harvest of wheat. The swollen sheaves swayed gently, promisingly, in the gentle breeze, swishing softly to and fro. It felt good to be alive!

They walked along in silence, drinking in the serenity of their pastoral surrounding when suddenly the father turned to his son, saying, "Just look at the marvel of Nature! See how *Hashem* has a plan and a purpose for every single stalk of wheat, every puff of wind, the swaying of each blade of grass! Everything is included in *Hashem*'s overall master plan of creation! Is it not marvelous that One so exalted and mighty should consider every tiny, minute speck on this world?!"

They continued along the country road, breathing in the fresh air, each one silent with his own thoughts. Soon they came to a forest and continued walking leisurely among the trees. Engrossed in his thoughts, R'

Yosef Yitzchak absent-mindedly plucked a leaf off a branch. He held the leaf in his hand and from time to time would unconsciously tear off a bit and throw it away.

His father noticed what he was doing and commented, "I don't understand how you can do something destructive like that without thinking. Don't you know that even a leaf is part of creation, that it has its purpose? Did I not just tell you how *Hashem* guides the destiny of every tiny thing, even a leaf? Don't you realize that a leaf is also a living thing; it breathes and grows. Why is the 'I' of a leaf any different than the 'I' of a human being? To be sure, you can think and speak while it is only a plant. Still, just as you, a human being, have a task to fill in this world, so does this leaf have a purpose to accomplish during its lifetime on this world!"

Wartime Decorations

אַתֶּם עֵדַי

You are My witnesses
(Haftorah Parashas Bereishis, Yeshayahu 43)
This can be read as deriving from the root 'adi' — jewel
and adornment. Hashem bedecks Himself, as it were, with
Bnei Yisrael

(Writings)

It was the Gerrer Rebbe's last year. The author of the famous *Sefas Emes* was already elderly when war broke out between Russia and Japan. Many of his devoted followers were drafted for military service and sent to the front lines.

The Rebbe could not be with them in body. But he certainly was with them in spirit, suffering along as if he, too, squatted in the trenches. He did not sleep in his comfortable bed but lay on the floor, on top of a tear-drenched robe. For the Rebbe never went to sleep without shedding many tears and offering many prayers for the safety of his chasidim at the front.

The chasidim surely felt it. They kept in close contact with the Rebbe by mail, reassuring him that they had not forgotten all that he had instilled in them, especially the importance of Torah study at all times. Whenever they had a chance, they would note the original ideas — the *chiddushim* — which had struck them during their haphazard study, also sending the latest news of the military progress at the front lines.

The Rebbe read their letters and was encouraged. One letter in particular brought him deep satisfaction. It was a long discussion, a complex *pilpul* written almost under direct enemy fire, right from the battle front, by a devout follower, R' Meir of Ostrovtza.

The Rebbe read this letter over and over again, cherishing it like a precious possession. He hastened to send a reply which opened thus, "'I have called upon the heavens and earth to testify...' (*Devarim* 30:19) The word 'testify — *ha'idosi'* can also be derived from the root *adi* — adornment. *Hashem* says that He adorns His heavens and His earth with Jews such as you..."

פָּרָשַׁת נֹחַ

Parashas Noach

The Faithful Shepherd

וַיִּזְכֹּר אֱ-לֹהִים אֶת נֹחַ וְאֵת כָּל הַחַיָּה וְאֶת כָּל הַבְּהֵמָה
And G-d remembered Noach and all the beasts and all the
animals (8:1)

In his youth, King David tended his father's sheep. Each day he took his flock far into the desert so that they would not eat from other people's pastures.

David, the shepherd, watched devotedly over the sheep and goats. He noticed that the large, strong animals pushed the weaker ones aside and took the most tender grass for themselves. When they had finished feeding, all that remained for the weaker sheep and goats was the leftover tough grass and weeds which they could not even bite with their weaker teeth.

"This is not right!" thought David. "It is not fair for the stronger animals to eat the best grass. With their stronger teeth, they should be eating the tougher stalks and leaving the tender blades for the weaker ones!"

David decided to do something about it. He built three pens: one was for the older, weaker sheep and goats, one for the young kids and lambs, and a third for the strong, robust animals.

Each morning, David would first open the pen that held the young lambs and kids and let them graze upon the soft, juicy grass. They rushed out, gratefully pouncing upon the food. They ate until they had their fill.

He led them back to their pen and released the old and feeble animals and let them graze next. The grass that was left was not too tough for their teeth. They, too, ate until they were satisfied.

By now, only the tougher stalks and roots remained. But the strong sheep were able to get at these with their hardy teeth and so, they also had enough to eat.

Thus, each group ate the food that suited it best and the entire flock was satisfied and healthy.

When *Hashem* noted this, He said, "One who knows how to care for his sheep so intelligently and well will make a perfect shepherd for My sheep too! Let him come and watch over Israel!"

That is how David was chosen to become king over Israel.

(According to *Midrash Rabba Shemos* 2:2)

Kindness to Animals

וַיִּזְכֹּר אֱ-לֹהִים אֶת נֹחַ וְאֵת כָּל הַחַיָּה וְאֵת כָּל הַבְּהֵמָה
And G-d remembered Noach and all the beasts and all the animals (8:1)

R'Yehudah Hanasi was the prince, or leader, of Jewry. The people loved this saintly and holy leader and used to call him *Rabbenu Hakadosh*, or simply,

Rebbe.

Day after day, Rebbe used to sit and teach the many students who flocked to him. One day, they were all seated outside in front of the *beis haknesses* studying together.

Just then some men walked by leading a young calf. They were taking it to the *shochet* to be slaughtered for a festive meal.

Suddenly, just as they reached the synagogue, the calf bolted and ran towards Rebbe. It burrowed under his cloak, trying to find shelter. "Moo, moo!" it lowed plaintively, as if begging Rebbe to save him.

But Rebbe was deeply engrossed in his study and did not take pity on the animal. He removed it from under his cloak and said, "How can I help you? Go, for that is what you were created for! Cows and calves were created to provide people with meat."

From that day on, Rebbe suffered terribly from a toothache. For thirteen years he suffered. No doctor was able to cure him or to alleviate his pain — for this was *Hashem*'s will.

Thirteen years later, Rebbe's maid, while cleaning the house one day, found some baby weasels hiding in a corner and wanted to sweep them outside where they belonged.

"Leave them be," Rebbe begged her. "Does it not say in *Tehillim* 'His mercy is upon all of His creatures'? *Hashem* has pity on all living things, even upon these tiny, insignificant and helpless beings.

Hashem heard this and decreed, "Now that Rebbe has shown compassion upon living creatures, the time has come for Me to take pity on him!"

On that very day Rebbe stopped suffering from his toothache.

(From Tractate *Bava Metzia* 85: *Midrash Rabba Bereishis* 33:3)

Where is R' David?

וַיִּזְכֹּר אֱ־לֹהִים אֶת נֹחַ וְאֵת כָּל הַחַיָּה וְאֶת כָּל הַבְּהֵמָה

And G-d remembered Noach and all the beasts and all the animals (8:1)

It was the eve of *Rosh Hashanah*. Everyone had had a busy day, preparing for the holy festival. But now that evening had fallen, everyone was in the *beis haknesses* in Lublin, waiting for the service to begin.

The Chozeh of Lublin looked around at the packed hall. One person was noticeably missing. It was R' David of Lelov, the great *tzaddik* who would be spending this festival in Lublin. "We cannot start without R' David!" said the Chozeh emphatically. "Send someone out to look for him."

The chasidim rushed out to search. What could be detaining the great man on this important evening? They finally found him after much searching. To their surprise, he was standing beside a horse, feeding him oats from his own hat!

"What are you doing?" they asked in wonder.

"The horse's owner must have worked the beast very hard today. It is starving. And yet, he forgot to feed him before going to *shul*."

A man must pray, but a hungry horse still comes first.

The Vanished Rainbow

וְהָיָה בְּעַנְנִי עָנָן... וְנִרְאֲתָה הַקֶּשֶׁת בֶּעָנָן

And it shall be when I bring clouds over the earth and the rainbow will be seen in the cloud (9:14)

R' Yehoshua ben Levi was an exceptionally holy man, one who even had the privilege of studying Torah with Eliyahu Hanavi! One time, in the midst of their study, the two came upon a difficult passage, a law that R' Shimon bar Yochai had taught. R' Yehoshua could not understand it.

Eliyahu Hanavi then suggested, "Would you like to speak to R' Shimon yourself? Wait! I will take you to him."

The two went to the tomb of R' Shimon bar Yochai on Mount Meron. Eliyahu called out, asking the *tana* to appear.

A voice called back from within the tomb. "Who is with you?"

"R' Yehoshua ben Levi," the prophet replied. "He has come to ask you a *halachic* question."

R' Shimon refused to reply.

Eliyahu defended R' Yehoshua's greatness and said, "But he is a leader of his generation. He is a true *tzaddik!*"

R' Shimon wished to make sure. "Did a rainbow ever appear in the sky during his lifetime?"

"Yes," R' Yehoshua admitted.

R' Shimon said: "If he had been a true *tzaddik* — a rainbow would not have appeared in his lifetime. I refuse to speak to him."

Throughout the lifetime of R' Shimon bar Yochai no rainbow ever appeared in the sky, because he was so righteous.

Our Sages explained that, in truth, no rainbow was seen in R' Yehoshua's lifetime either but he was so humble that he did not wish to boast and so did not reveal this to R' Shimon bar Yochai.

The rainbow is an unfavorable sign, even though it is so beautiful, because it reminds us of *Hashem*'s promise to Noach that He would never destroy the world again. When people on earth make *Hashem* angry and He brings storms and destructive rains, He is reminded of His promise not to flood the earth by the rainbow in the sky. If there is a *tzaddik* in the generation, however, this sign is unnecessary for *Hashem* does not get angry with His people, because of that great man's merit!

(According to *Midrash Rabba, Bereishis 35; Yalkut Shimoni, Bereishis Siman 61*)

"Someone Is Looking!"

וַיֵּרֶד ה' לִרְאוֹת
And Hashem descended to see (11:5)

R' Yosef Zundel of Salant had business to take care of at the annual fair and hired a wagon to take him there.

As they were driving along a deserted country road, the wagoner noticed a large pile of hay in the middle of a field. This is just what he needed for his horse. It would save him the cost of a few meals. He quickly grabbed a large sack from under his seat, ran out to the middle of the field and began stuffing it with hay. Suddenly he heard his passenger warning him, "Someone's looking! Someone's looking!"

The wagoner turned his sack upside down and quickly shook out all the hay, and in the wink of an eye was back on the wagon. He flicked the reins and they were on their way.

When he had recovered from the scare, the driver looked around. The scene was as bare as before. There was not a soul in sight!

"Hey! You fooled me! There's no one looking!"

"Trick you?! G-d forbid!" said the rabbi, offended at being thus accused. "I was telling the honest truth; someone *was* watching!"

"Who? I don't see a single soul for miles around!"

"You mean a person? No, there are no people around here," R' Yosef Zundel admitted. "But up there," he pointed to the sky, "in heaven there is a watchful eye and a listening ear that are constantly on guard and all your deeds are recorded."

A Sigh and a Smile

בְּרֶגַע קָטֹן עֲזַבְתִּיךְ וּבְרַחֲמִים גְּדֹלִים אֲקַבְּצֵךְ

*For a small moment have I forsaken you but with great
compassion will I gather you
(Haftorah Parashas Noach, Yeshayahu 54)*

R'Saadya was the *rosh yeshivah* of the world famous
Sura Yeshivah of *Bavel*. His home was like a royal
palace. It also was a beacon for Jewry the world over.
From this majestic home R' Saadya led the affairs of
Babylonian Jewry, his light casting its glow to the far
corners of the globe.

It was the month of *Nisan*. Jews all over the world
were frantically busy, cleaning their homes of all traces of
chametz. In the home of R' Saadya, activity was at its
peak. Walls and windows were being washed down, nooks
and crannies inspected, old furniture disposed of to make
way for new, luxurious fittings.

One of R' Saadya's trusty servants was by the
riverside, immersing new dishes into the river as the
halachah required, before they could be used in a Jewish
household. R' Saadya had bought a beautiful set of
crystalware in honor of the coming Festival of Liberation
when everyone is supposed to feel like a king. The
servant had placed them all in a basket and was about to
dip them into the river, one by one, when suddenly a
mighty wave arose, sweeping all the precious vessels into
the water.

The servant watched helplessly as they sank to the

bottom. It certainly had not been his fault! What would they say back at the mansion when they found out? Could he hide it? He mulled the matter over in his mind, wondering what to do. "They might not even miss this particular set. The master has many crystal dishes, similar to these. And even if he does miss them, he will not be able to trace anything back to me. No one will be able to point an accusing finger at me. Besides, I am not really to blame. It was an act of G-d. It could have happened to anyone just as well."

The servant convinced himself that no one would know the difference — and continued immersing the rest of the new dishes. He finished the task and returned home.

It was just as he had predicted. No one missed the dishes. In time, even the servant almost forgot the incident.

The year passed and it was *Nisan* again. The same servant was sent again to dip the new things into the river to make them permissible for use. Suddenly, he remembered the calamity of the previous year, which he had kept secret. He was suddenly afraid that the same thing would happen this year as well.

He drew near the river bank carefully and looked at the swirling water. The river was swollen with melted winter snows and it rushed madly by, its high waves pounding the shores. The servant stood at the same spot as the previous year and looked down. Suddenly he noticed something floating to the surface, towards him. He stretched out his hand and grabbed it. It was a crystal dish. And there was another, and another. He fished them out of the water one by one. It was the very set which had fallen in last year! Not a single item was missing! How strange that the river should cough them up after having buried them for an entire year and deliver them at his very feet. Surely this was no chance coincidence! It must mean something.

The servant resolved to tell his master the entire story when he reached home. It would not be easy since his role in the matter was not too honorable. For, even if he were not to blame, still, he had kept the matter to himself. Nevertheless, he was curious to hear what the sage had to say about the strange coincidence.

Gathering his courage, he knocked on the rabbi's study and was told to enter. Clasping his hands in front of him humbly, he unfolded the strange story and his guilty part in it. His voice lifted when he told how he had retrieved the dishes from the river and he concluded, "Fortune smiles brightly on the rabbi, if he is able to reclaim such precious articles from a raging river." He expected his master to rejoice along with him.

But no! Instead of smiling, R' Saadya began scowling. An ominous black look crept over his face and a heavy sigh escaped his throat.

What was the matter? The servant dared not ask. Thinking that his master was angry at him, the servant crept silently out of the room and closed the door after him.

Within a short time R' Saadya lost all of his wealth. His creditors came, demanding to be paid, but he had nothing with which to pay them. His costly furnishings and magnificent possessions were auctioned off and his mansion sold to cover his debts. He was left with nothing more than the clothing on his back. All of his servants went to find themselves new masters, leaving R' Saadya, the famous *rosh yeshivah*, penniless. His family was forced to accept communal charity and he was driven to wander from place to place seeking ways to support himself and his family.

As for the servant who had witnessed the strange return of the crystal dishes, he, also, left his master and went to seek his fortune in Egypt. He invested the little money he had saved in business and soon became very wealthy.

In his travels, R' Saadya reached the city where his former servant now lived as a prosperous and prominent citizen. R' Saadya roamed the streets, his clothes tattered, his eyes deeply sunken in a pale face. As he was standing forlornly in the middle of the marketplace a man suddenly ran up to him, embraced him warmly and said, "Rebbe! Master! What has become of you!" It was the former servant. Despite the ravages of time and misfortune, he had recognized R' Saadya. R' Saadya told him briefly of all that had happened to him and the former servant said, "You must come home with me, Rebbe! You must come and live with me until times get better for you. *Hashem* has blessed me with everything and now that I can, I wish to repay you for the kindness I knew in your home, in small measure, at least. You can devote yourself to Torah study, as you once did, without any worries or cares. Please, you will be doing me the greatest honor!"

R' Saadya could not refuse such a warm invitation. Besides he was in no position to refuse. He had no home, nothing. He was on the verge of starvation, of physical collapse. This offer had come just at the right moment.

A special room was set aside for R' Saadya, furnished with all the comforts he could dream of. But he was not as yet to enjoy release from trouble. Providence had not yet decreed an end to his suffering. The following morning found R' Saadya very ill, struck down by a raging fever and an overpowering weakness. The suffering of these last years had finally caught up with him. He lay there delirious, oblivious of his surroundings.

The faithful servant-turned-rich-man hovered over him solicitously. He immediately called his doctor but the latter said that only time would tell; the patient was really too weak to fight his fever. The host called in a better doctor but his prognosis was the same. R' Saadya's life was in the hands of *Hashem*.

The faithful host hovered over his guest day and night, trying to ease his suffering, bathing his burning forehead, wetting his lips. He tried to get him to eat but R' Saadya was too weak for that. Slowly the little strength he had dwindled away until he was a mere shadow on the bed.

In his desperation, the good host called in the best doctor in the country. He, too, was discouraging. But he did offer some advice.

"Boil up several fat chickens in a large pot for many hours. Let the soup simmer down to a mere essence. Take this essence and reduce it to one spoonful. This spoonful should have great restorative powers. If the patient eats this one spoon of chicken essence, he has a chance of getting better."

The host was overjoyed that there was something specific that he could do. He himself went to the market to select the finest pullets there were, plump, juicy birds whose own vitality would be transferred to R' Saadya to guide him over the crisis.

The chickens were properly *kashered*; they were plopped into a huge pot and put on the fire. A heavenly smell of rich chicken soup filled the house, making every one's mouth water — except that of the patient, who had no appetite, no strength to go on living. All that day the chickens simmered until all the rich juices were concentrated. Then this sauce was reduced until nothing remained but one spoonful of golden, life-giving liquid.

The good host himself hastened to bring this precious soup to R' Saadya. But just as he was lifting it to the patient's mouth a spider web fell from the ceiling, right into the spoon, rendering it unfit for eating. All those hours of work...

A cry went up throughout the household. Everyone had had their hopes pinned on this precious soup. Everyone wanted to see the great sage recover. And now, all that labor — for nothing. In vain!

The host lowered his eyes. He was too pained to look at R' Saadya. Would he have to begin all over again? Would the dying man live long enough for fresh soup to be prepared? Who knows what might happen this time? He was about to weep when something compelled him to look at the patient.

R' Saadya was smiling!

Everyone in tears and R' Saadya, whose life hung in the balance, smiling!

Suddenly another scene flashed through his memory. When he had told his master of the lost crystalware and how they had returned so miraculously, raised up by the river current, R' Saadya should have rejoiced at having regained his precious vessels, yet then he had scowled. And now, when he lay on his deathbed, his very last hopes dashed to the ground, he was smiling! What did all this mean?

He could contain himself no longer. Bending over the sick man so that R' Saadya need not strain himself to speak, the host said, "Rebbe, I beg of you, please explain the two things that puzzle me. Why, when I told you about the valuable things which had come back, did you sigh and frown when you should have rejoiced? And now, after so much effort had been put into making the one remedy that might save your life and that effort was in vain, why did you smile? What is the significance of such strange behavior?"

R' Saadya continued smiling. In a weak whisper, he explained, "Just as no one is immune to misfortune, so is no one so hopeless that nothing can help him. Everyone has his ups and downs. The wheel of fortune revolves; one time a person is up, another time he is down. But the lower a person falls, the closer he is to rising and vice versa. When you told me about the valuable crystalware which had so unnaturally come back to me, I was wary. No person is so lucky that everything always goes well. This must be a sign that I had finally reached the peak of my success, of my good fortune. The descent would now begin for I could not remain on top. Indeed, that is precisely when I began losing my money. From that time on, everything went wrong. I plunged lower and lower. And as if this were not enough, even when I had the good fortune to meet you, my troubles were still not over for I became ill. Then, to make things all the worse, the very slim chance of my recovery — eating that spoonful of life-giving liquid — was dashed to the ground. Could anyone be in more hopeless a situation than this? You see me now at the very nadir, the low point, of my life, with one foot in the grave. But since I cannot fall any lower, I will have to ascend. This is the sign that my fortune will begin improving for it certainly cannot get any worse! Now you understand why I smile."

And so it was. During the next few days a remarkable

change took place. R' Saadya began eating and gathered strength. Soon he was able to leave his bed and walk around. Within a month he felt full of vigor, ready to return home to Sura.

Here, fortune again looked up on him. He was able to pay off his debts, go into business and regain the wealth and status which he had once enjoyed. He was, again, the *Gaon*, the pride and leader of Israel.

The Wondrous Tavernkeeper

וְכָל בָּנַיִךְ לִמּוּדֵי ה'... בִּצְדָקָה תִּכּוֹנָנִי

And all of your children shall be taught of Hashem... in righteousness shall you be established
(Haftorah Parashas Noach, Yeshayahu 54)

It was difficult to believe, by merely looking at him, that the Jewish tavernkeeper was really a holy man, a miracle worker. It was hard to believe that when this plainly dressed, almost coarse, peasantlike man blessed someone the blessing was almost always fulfilled! And yet that was what happened, time after time.

The villagers all knew this to be true and deeply respected the innkeeper. And soon his reputation spread all over the countryside. When the Rebbe of Apta, who was then living in Mezibuz, heard about this man, he was curious to meet him. If he was a simple man, from where did his wondrous power come? What could he, the Rebbe of Apta, learn from him?

The only way to learn was to go there.

When he was face to face with the tavernkeeper, the Rebbe of Apta was not impressed by his outward appearance. He watched him for a while but still could not see anything special about the man's behavior. Finally he begged, "Please tell me, what is the secret of your wonderful powers? What special trait do you possess that is so favored in heaven that all of your blessings are fulfilled?"

"My powers come from my unshakeable faith in *Hashem*," he said simply, modestly.

"Tell me more about yourself," the Rebbe begged.

"I have always had faith in *Hashem*. Whatever happened to me, I always trusted that it would be for the best since it came from *Hashem*. And if things looked bad, I never despaired, knowing that with the help of *Hashem*, everything would turn out all right in the end. I also gave much *tzedakah*, especially during difficult times. I always gave generously to those who had less than I.

"In addition, I always kept an open house for wayfarers. I welcomed guests and treated them royally. One time, as I was entertaining some travelers, there came a sudden knock at the door. It was a messenger from my landlord. He wanted me to appear before him at once. He threatened to throw me into prison if I did not come immediately.

"I did not know what to do. I still had my hungry guests to feed. They had come from afar and if I did not give them to eat they would go to bed hungry and would not wait for my return. I made a quick decision. I would do what my conscience told me to do and leave the problem of the landlord up to *Hashem.* I put my trust in Him that everything would turn out all right.

"I took care of my guests, making sure that they ate and drank. Then I showed them to their rooms. Only afterwards did I allow myself to obey the landlord's summons, hours after it had been delivered.

"I found him all smiles. For no particular reason at all, his mood had suddenly changed and he greeted me warmly. He did not throw me into jail. Everything had worked out fine after all.

"This is only one example. Actually, everything always works out all right, as long as I keep on trusting in *Hashem.* And so I no longer worry, no matter how bleak things may appear.

"Two years ago, I suddenly lost all of my possessions. Nothing remained of my wealth, not even a penny. But do you think that I was upset or anxious? Not in the least. My family's faith is not as strong as mine. They kept on pressing me to do something. They urged me to go to the nearest city and find a businessman willing to invest his money with me and become a partner. They saw this as the only practical way out.

"I did not relish this idea. I preferred remaining independent. Why should I suddenly begin relying on flesh-and-blood when all along I had trusted in *Hashem* and had not been disappointed? I argued back but was one against many. In the end I gave in and went to the city.

"As I traveled along the road, passing over lush green fields, orchards heavy with fruit, vineyards bursting with luscious grapes and cows grazing peacefully at pasture, my faith in *Hashem* became stronger than ever. If He could create such a beautiful world and sustain it, day after day, could He not support me and my family? Why must I begin putting my trust in mankind when I could trust *Hashem*, Who had created all mankind? Why should I not go directly to the source of all life and all livelihood? And from the depths of my heart a prayer welled up, 'Hashem! You are the Master of the world, the Sustainer of living things! Listen to my plea. I am in trouble. I have lost all of my money and am penniless. I cannot continue running my tavern for I cannot buy new merchandise. My family tells me to take in a partner. But why should I place my trust in a human being who is here today and gone tomorrow? *Hashem*, why can't You be my partner? Let me make You an offer. We will split everything evenly down the middle. I will give You half of everything I earn. Half for You; half for me. I will distribute Your half among the poor, among Torah scholars and use my half to support my own family.'

"As soon as I had said these words I felt better. Suddenly I felt something hard in my pocket. I thrust my hand in and there was a coin. I knew for sure that it had not been there before. How I had searched all of my pockets for every last coin... I looked at it. It was pure silver! I had never owned such a coin. This, then, was the answer to my prayer. My business offer had been accepted!

"I turned the wagon around and went back home. When I entered, I tossed the gleaming coin up in the air. 'Here,' I said. 'I found a partner for the business. This is his first installment.'

"The coin was enough to get me started again. I bought a small supply of liquor and sold it quickly, putting half of the profit aside right away for my 'partner'. And since then, that is what I have always done — set aside half of the profits in a special cashbox under my counter. I don't let anyone handle any of the money. No one knows who my partner is. And I handle His money as carefully as I do mine, even more so, for I must distribute it wisely where it will do the most good. This, then, is my story."

The Rebbe of Apta had been listening intently all the while. When the tavernkeeper had finished, he rose, thanked him and left.

When he returned to his own *beis medrash* in Mezibuz the Rebbe related all that he had heard to his chasidim, adding, "Whoever enters partnership with *Hashem* and is scrupulously honest in his dealings — is blessed with the power of performing wonders!"

After Six Years

בְּצְדָקָה תִּכּוֹנָנִי

*In righteousness shall you be established
(Haftorah Parashas Noach, Yeshayahu 54)*

There was once a couple, a man and wife, who, though virtuous and G-d fearing people, lived in dire poverty. The man worked very hard as a day laborer, earning very little money.

One time, as he was busy in the fields, an Arab appeared before him and greeted him. This man was none other than Eliyahu Hanavi in disguise but the Jew did not know this. He returned the stranger's greeting and went back to work.

Eliyahu Hanavi spoke again, saying, "*Hashem* knows of your dire poverty and wishes to grant you six years of prosperity and wealth. You will be able to buy whatever your heart desires once you are rich. When do you want these years? Now? Or at some later time?"

The man did not believe the Arab and so, replied, "Please, leave me alone and let me work."

Eliyahu Hanavi turned and went his way. But on the morrow, when the man was busy plowing he appeared to him again in the form of an Arab and asked, "*Hashem* wishes to grant you six good years. When do you want them?"

The worker disregarded the offer, as he had the day before, and said, "I do not believe you. Go away and don't bother me. I have work to do."

But when Eliyahu Hanavi appeared on the third day, the Jew understood that there was something to what he was saying. He therefore said, "Wait here. I will go and ask my wife."

He hurried home and told his wife about the three visits and the offer of the six years of great wealth. He asked her what he should do.

She advised, "Ask *Hashem* to grant the good years right away."

The worker returned to the field and found Eliyahu Hanavi waiting for his reply. He said, "We want the good years immediately."

"Very well," said the Arab. "Go home. You will see

that *Hashem* has already blessed you!"

The poor man's children had been playing outside in the sand, in their front yard. Suddenly, while they were digging innocently, they discovered a chest full of silver coins. They rushed to their mother and showed her what they had found.

The laborer was returning home just at this time. He saw his children holding a treasure chest in their hands and took it from them. Spreading its contents out on the table inside his hut, he saw that there was enough money there to last them for exactly six years! The family thanked *Hashem* for His great kindness and rejoiced together.

The man turned to his wife, asking, "What are we to do with this huge sum of money?"

She replied, "Let us only take as much as we require for our own basic, urgent needs, leaving the rest to distribute for worthy causes."

She immediately sent her small son to buy a notebook. From then on, each day he would jot down all the sums which they gave to the poor.

Thus did the six years pass.

At the end of the six good years Eliyahu Hanavi came to the Jew and said, "The time has come for you to give back everything that *Hashem* gave you."

He said, "I must first tell my wife." He rushed home and told his wife that the same Arab who had visited them six years ago had now come to reclaim the money.

"Go!" she said. "Tell him that if he can find people who can manage the money better than we have — he should give it to them!"

Hashem — Who knows what is hidden from human sight — knew all the good that the couple had done with the money He had given them. He therefore told Eliyahu not to take away their wealth. Furthermore, He told him to add on to their riches many times so that they could continue their good works for the rest of their lives.

(According to *Yalkut Shimoni Rus 607*)

פָּרָשַׁת לֶךְ־לְךָ

Parashas Lech Lecha

The Curse of Gold

לְזַרְעֲךָ אֶתֵּן אֶת הָאָרֶץ הַזֹּאת

To your seed will I give this land (12:7)

When Avraham was traveling through Aram Naharayim and Aram Nachor — he saw the people eating, drinking and leading idle lives. He said: 'I hope that my portion will not be in this land.' When he reached 'Eretz Yisrael' — he saw the people working industriously and said: 'I hope that my portion will be in this land!' Hashem said to him: 'To your seed will I give this land.'

(Midrash Rabba)

The following story was told by R' Yosef Chaim of *Bavel*, better known as the Ben Ish Chai:

Yechezkel was a woodchopper. His father and grandfather before him had been woodchoppers and most probably his children would be woodchoppers. It was not easy work. Yechezkel had to rise early each morning and go to the forest. Here he would chop wood all morning. When the sun was overhead, he would tie up the wood into convenient bundles and take them to town to sell for firewood. Whatever he earned that day went to feed his wife and children. Nothing remained for a rainy day or for a better future.

One day, in the heat of summer, he went to the forest as usual to chop his daily amount of firewood. Even there it was scorching. Each time he lifted his ax it became increasingly difficult. Sweat poured down his back. By midday he was completely exhausted.

"Is it the heat or am I getting old? Will things never change? Will life always be so difficult?" he asked himself. He bent over to tie the sticks together. He was about to lift them to his back and begin walking home when he changed his mind.

"It is much too hot to walk in the blazing sun. If I take a nap, under this tree, I will be able to walk twice as fast when I get up, for I will be refreshed."

He looked at the bundles of wood bitterly. They symbolized his fate. "Why am I such an unlucky man?" he thought. "Why must I work ceaselessly and not see any blessing in my labor? What do I have from life. A few limp vegetables at the end of the day to eat with a dry crust of bread?! Will I never be able to afford meat at my table? Never? Will I never know the taste of an apple, an orange, a banana? Why must I struggle so hard and get so little in return? It is not fair! Will I never feel the shiny hardness of a gold coin, only of small copper pennies? Why, *Hashem*? Tell me, why?"

No one was there to see, so he let his tears fall. Exhausted by work and tears, he leaned back against a tree trunk and fell asleep.

He slept and had a dream. In his dream a handsome young lad appeared before him, holding a golden scepter in his hand. He was fair, with a noble forehead and beautiful eyes. When he smiled, it seemed like the sun was shining forth in full luster. The youth spoke: "*Hashem* has heard your sigh of woe and has sent me to

grant any one wish that you make..." The poor woodchopper did not even hesitate. He blurted out: "I want everything that I touch to turn to gold!" "Very well, so be it!" said the youth. He touched the woodchopper with his golden scepter and then disappeared.

The man realized that this had been a heavenly angel sent to help him. He was overjoyed. No longer would he and his family have to starve. They would be rich, if everything that he touched turned to gold. To test his new powers he touched a log from his bundle of firewood. And lo! It turned to pure gold. A gold log!

"How wonderful!" the man exulted. "Now I need not even be a woodchopper. I can live a life of leisure! Let others do this lowly job. I am finished for life! I will build myself a mansion, hire servants and wear silk clothing just like the best of the nobility! All I need to do if I want money is to touch a stone, a stick, a clod of earth — and it will turn to gold! Who can compare to me? I will be the richest person in the entire land! Will there be any king to compare with me in riches?!"

He got up and stretched, feeling refreshed after his nap. He reached over to take a sip from his water canteen, for it was hot. But as soon as he touched it, it turned to gold! How wonderful! He tipped it to his lips to drink. But no water came out! What had happened? The water had touched his lips and turned to gold. He turned to his knapsack to take out some bread but that, too, turned to gold.

Suddenly he realized how foolish he had been. He had been so eager for riches that he had forgotten to what ridiculous lengths one would go and what damage a love for gold could bring. "What a fool I have been! What have I done? I will starve to death. Everything I touch will turn to gold and I will not be able to eat or drink anything! I have sold my soul for gold! But of what use will it be to me if I die of starvation? How will I enjoy my fortune? How much better it was when I labored for my daily bread — and was able to enjoy it!"

The man burst out crying — and woke up. It had all been a dream He looked all around him, at his bundle of firewood, at his knapsack and his canteen. Everything was just as he had left it! Nothing had changed. Nothing had turned to gold. How thankful he was!

"It was all a dream. But it was meant to teach me a deep lesson. I must learn to be satisfied with my lot, to be grateful that I have work that feeds me and my family. I must no longer envy those with riches, for they are not neccessarily any happier than I!"

A Bad and Bitter End

וַיְנַגַּע ה' אֶת פַּרְעֹה... וְאֶת בֵּיתוֹ עַל דְּבַר שָׂרָי

Hashem afflicted Pharaoh... and his house because of Sarai
(12:17)

A prominent man of Tzipori once invited R' Shimon ben Chalafta to his son's *bris*.

On the designated day R' Shimon traveled to Tzipori. As he arrived at the city gates, he was stopped by a group of wild street youths, brothers, playing in a courtyard. They wanted to make sport of the distinguished looking Jew and demanded that he dance for them.

"But I am an old man! It is not fitting to ask me to dance for you!" he replied. They refused to let him go.

R' Shimon raised his eyes towards heaven and saw, in his divine intuition, that it was decreed from heaven that the very courtyard where they were playing was to be destroyed. With this in mind, he turned to the youths and said, "Very well. I will sing for you but you must do what I tell you. You must go to the owner of this courtyard. If he is asleep, wake him up and say this to him: The beginning of sin is sweet but its end is bad and bitter."

He meant that a father who does not educate his son, who does not watch over him and punish him, who does not instill wisdom, *mussar* and good sense — will reap a bitter end!

The conversation woke up the owner of the courtyard, who had been sleeping. He heard and understood. Rushing outside, he fell at R' Shimon's feet, weeping, "Please pay no attention to them. They are only foolish youngsters!"

R' Shimon replied, "What shall I do? The decree has already been sealed; your house is to be destroyed. But I can do this for you: Take everything out of the house; it shall not be destroyed until you have removed whatever you wish to save!"

The owner rushed back into the house and began taking out all of his furniture and possessions. The minute he finished, the house collapsed and the courtyard was a hill of ruins.

(According to *Midrash Rabba Koheles* 3:4)

Unshakeable Faith

וְהֶאֱמִין בַּה'

And he trusted in Hashem (15:6)

W hat lesson did the Rebbe, the Baal Shem Tov, wish to impart to them this time, the chasidim wondered, as they were gathered together and told to climb into the coach. This was to be another wonderful ride which would give them new insight into the strange and marvelous ways of *Hashem* or into the greatness of His chosen people, the Jews, whose simplest folk were capable of acts of deep love and faith.

As usual, the horses were given free rein. Once out of Mezibuz, they lifted their hoofs and began flying over hills and valleys, through towns and villages, towards some unknown destination.

The chasidim sat inside the coach; the Rebbe was speaking. He was telling them about the Divine Providence of *Hashem* over every single creature in the world. From His exalted throne in heaven, He saw and guided everything that went on down below. Nothing escaped *Hashem's* attention. Nothing was too small or too insignificant...

The chasidim listened carefully to this deep lesson. They were certain it would soon be applied through a true happening, something that had to do with this trip. They thought about the Rebbe's words and did not notice where they were going.

After many hours of travel the coach stopped in front

of an inn. The Jewish innkeeper rushed outside, welcoming in his guests with warmth and joy. He hastened to put some refreshments before them on the table. While he was busy serving the chasidim, there were three knocks on the window. These were followed by three knocks on the door. A gentile walked boldly in, knocked three times on the wooden table and left as strangely as he had come.

"What is the meaning of this strange behavior?" the Baal Shem Tov asked the innkeeper.

"Oh, that is the landlord's messenger. That is his way of reminding me that today my rent is due. I pay once a year. If I do not have the money by evening, he will send his soldiers to arrest me. Then I will have to sit in jail until I pay up my debt."

"You do not seem very upset about it," the Baal Shem Tov commented. "You probably have the money all ready. Why don't you go and pay it, then? Don't worry about us. We will sit here and await your return."

"Oh, but you are wrong. I do not even have one cent of the year's rent in my pocket. This has been a very difficult year; I have had many expenses and few profits. But I am not very worried. I have faith in *Hashem* Who will not abandon a Jew in his time of trouble. Anyway, I have until tomorrow. Many things can happen until then. I am not afraid. Meanwhile, my honored guests, wash your hands and sit down to a hearty meal. I know that things will turn out all right."

The chasidim looked more concerned than the innkeeper! But when they saw the fine meal he had prepared and saw their Rebbe washing his hands, they also followed and sat down to a sumptuous meal.

When they came to the words in the *bircas hamazon*

asking *Hashem* to "send plentiful blessing to this house" the Baal Shem Tov closed his eyes in deep concentration. When he had finished, the chasidim answered *"Amen"* fervently.

Seeing that his guests no longer needed him, the landlord put on his *Shabbos* jacket and apologized for leaving. "I must go to the landlord now. You will forgive me, won't you?"

"But what will you do?" the Baal Shem Tov asked. "You do not have the money to pay. Surely you do not expect to return. He will throw you into jail."

The innkeeper smiled. "I am not worried. Something will come up. *Hashem* will rescue me somehow, I am sure."

The chasidim crowded in the doorway, marveling at his composure. The man was not even worried! How deep was the faith of this simple Jew! They had never seen anything to compare with it!

The man strode down the country road towards the landlord's luxurious mansion. What could possibly happen to save him in the few minutes before he reached his destination? They watched carefully.

Suddenly they saw a carriage roll up and stop right before the innkeeper. Its occupant, a wealthy looking man, stepped down and began speaking to the innkeeper. They conversed seriously for a few minutes, then the man climbed back inside the coach. The innkeeper continued walking down the road.

The man in the carriage seemed to have changed his mind, for a few minutes later he whipped his horses and had them overtake the walking man. He, again, stopped him and got down to discuss something earnestly with him. This time the rich man took out a purse and began counting out money into the innkeeper's hand. The innkeeper took the money and began walking towards the landlord's home. The rich man gave the signal to the horses and before long, the coach was speeding towards the inn. "Now our curiosity will be satisfied," the Baal Shem Tov said to his open-eyed chassidim.

The man rode up to the inn and then got out of his carriage. He entered the inn and sat down at a table. Turning to the group of chasidim, he said,

"What an amazing person that innkeeper is! I just stopped him before on the road to negotiate a sale. I wanted to buy my winter's supply of whiskey from his brewery. I know him to be an honest person, yet, I did not agree to his first price and I let him go his way. He told me he needed a certain amount to pay up his yearly rent and would not settle for anything less than that full sum. I thought it over and decided that the price he quoted was also a fair one and ran to overtake him. We made the deal there, on the road, and I paid up the entire sum in cash. It was just enough for his rent, he said. He had to go at once to pay it up, but asked me to go to his inn and wait for him."

The chasidim looked at one another. *Hashem* had answered the good Jew's prayers. He had not disappointed his deep faith, but, at the last minute, had provided the entire sum that he needed.

The Baal Shem Tov nodded, "See, that is the power of pure faith..."

They were now ready to return to Mezibuz. They had just learned a powerful lesson that day; one they would never forget.

At the Right Moment

וְהֶאֱמִין בַּה׳

And he trusted in Hashem (15:6)

The Baal Shem Tov and his disciple, R' Menachem Mendel of Ber, were walking along a deserted road. They were far from any signs of civilization; all was desolate, scorched by a hot summer sun. There was no water in sight, no farmhouse, no well.

"What are we going to do? We will die of thirst!" R' Menachem Mendel said desperately.

"Where is your faith in *Hashem*, your *bitachon*?" the Baal Shem Tov chided his disciple. "Your faith has to be strong enough for you to believe in miracles. If you really and truly have faith that *Hashem* can provide us with water, even in this deserted, desolate spot, if you believe with your heart and soul, then He truly will! Now begin to concentrate!"

R' Menachem Mendel closed his eyes tightly and thought deeply. Finally he opened his eyes and said, "*Hashem* can surely provide us with water, even in this forsaken spot."

Suddenly, a gentile appeared, as if from nowhere. "Have you perhaps seen horses roaming about? They have run away from me. I have been looking for them for the past three days but have found no trace of them."

The two men shook their heads. "No, we are sorry, but we have seen no horses here. They must have gone in a different direction."

The gentile was about to turn around when suddenly a thought struck him, "You look like you are very thirsty. Would you like some water? Here, I have a pitcher full, much more than I need. Drink your fill."

The two men tipped the water pitcher to their lips and drank until their thirst was quenched. Thanking the man, they continued along.

R' Menachem Mendel turned to his teacher and said, "I am now really convinced that faith can perform miracles. But there is one thing I do not understand. The man said that he had been wandering around this area for three days in search of his horses. I know that *Hashem* sent him especially to quench our thirst. Why, then, did he set out three days ago?"

The Baal Shem Tov replied, "*Hashem* expected us to be traveling through this area. He anticipated our thirst and wanted the water to be on hand at the very moment that we needed — and prayed — for it."

The True Doctor

וְהֶאֱמִן בַּה'

And he trusted in Hashem (15:6)

R' Yitzchak of Nishchiz was a holy man whose blessings came true. People flocked from near and far to beg the *tzaddik* to pray for them. He was especially famous for curing the ill. His impassioned prayers on behalf of all afflicted people went directly to heaven and were not refused.

The Rebbe loved his fellow Jews and prayed for them willingly. One time, however, when a man with a fatal illness came to him, he refused to pray for him.

"You may live or you may die. I cannot guarantee anything. I don't know if I can help you at all," said the Rebbe. The man was crestfallen. The Rebbe had been his last resort. He had gone to the best doctors, paid out huge sums. He could not understand why the Rebbe was so unsympathetic. This man knew of countless people who had been helped by the Rebbe's prayers. Why did he refuse to help him?!

"Do you want to know why I cannot pray for you?" the Rebbe finally said after an uncomfortable pause. "It is because you rely on me. You think that only I can help you. But you are wrong. You are the one who can help yourself. You must pray to *Hashem* and place your trust in Him. Only if you realize that your deliverance can come only from *Hashem* — can I help you. If you put your entire trust in me, a mere human being, then I can do nothing. Let me tell you a story:

A couple once came to R' Yisrael of Kozhnitz, who was also granted special powers to help people. They wanted him to help them find a great sum of money which they had lost.

"Bless us, Rebbe, that we may find the huge sum which we have lost," they begged. R' Yisrael refused. They were surprised. Whispering between themselves, they took out a gold coin and said, "Here, Rebbe, take this to distribute to the poor. But pray for us!" Still the Rebbe refused to help them. He sat back in his chair and said, "For sixty gold coins, perhaps, I will be able to help you." "Sixty gold coins!" the woman gasped. "For that amount we don't need you! We can pray to *Hashem* to help us!" She was about to take back the single gold coin that still lay on the table when R' Yisrael smiled at the couple, "*Now* I can help you. Now that you have put your trust in *Hashem*, I can also help you. But as long as you thought that only I could find your money, I was helpless. You must realize that I am only a small messenger of *Hashem* on earth, here to do His work. If you place your trust in Him, then I can use my powers to help you."

"Like that couple," concluded R' Yitzchak of Nishchiz, "you regarded me as another doctor, a miracle worker, perhaps, forgetting all about the genuine Doctor, the true Healer of all flesh."

A Fair Exchange?

וְהֶאֱמִן בַּה׳

And he trusted in Hashem (15:6)

A poor housepainter once listened to R' Yisrael Salant speak about the greatness of faith, of absolute trust in *Hashem*.

After R' Yisrael's sermon, he approached the great scholar and asked innocently, "If I put all my faith in *Hashem* that I will get ten thousand rubles, will it come true?"

"Most certainly!" said R' Yisrael fervently. "I am willing to guarantee it!"

Reassured by the *tzaddik's* word, the housepainter went home. In the following weeks he did not work but spent all of his time in the *beis medrash* saying *Tehillim*. Slowly his house became bare of food and money. When his family was on the verge of starvation, the man's wife insisted that he either go back to work or go to R' Yisrael and collect the money. He had guaranteed it, after all. The painter went to R' Yisrael.

"Rebbe," he complained. "I have put all of my faith in *Hashem* that He would reward me with ten thousand rubles. But I have not received even one! Meanwhile my family is starving and we have no money for food! What about your promise?!"

"I still firmly believe that if you put your full trust in *Hashem*, you will yet get that money," said R' Yisrael. "But if you wish, I will advance you five thousand rubles on the condition that when you get the ten thousand, you will give them all to me."

The painter nodded eagerly. "Rebbe, I agree!"

"Aha!" said R' Yisrael scornfully. "Your faith cannot be very strong if you are willing to exchange ten thousand rubles for half that amount. How then do you expect to get the ten thousand to begin with?! You need not expect anything!"

An Exchange

וּבֶן שְׁמֹנַת יָמִים יִמּוֹל לָכֶם כָּל זָכָר

At the age of eight days shall you circumcise to you every male (17:12)

The Roman emperor had passed a law forbidding all the Jews in the land of Israel to circumcise their sons. It was during this period that R' Yehudah Hanasi was born. He was to become so beloved that everyone would call him merely 'Rebbe' — our teacher'.

Rabban Shimon ben Gamliel, his father, said: "*Hashem* commanded us to circumcise our sons on the eighth day. The wicked Romans have decreed that we must not circumcise them. Whom should we obey? *Hashem* or the Roman emperor? *Hashem*, to be sure!!!"

He performed the *bris* at once.

The Romans found out and they rushed to inform the Roman governor who summoned Rabban Shimon ben Gamliel before him. "Why did you disobey the emperor's law and circumcise your son?" he asked.

"Our G-d ordered us to circumcise our sons," Rabban Shimon replied forthrightly. "We must obey His commandments first!"

"You are a prominent, respected person, the *Nasi* of Jewry. Still, I cannot overlook this! You blatantly defied the law!"

"What are you going to do about it?"

"I will have to send the circumcised child to the emperor. Let him decide what to do with you!" said the governor. He was certain that the emperor would punish the rebellious Jew severely.

Rabban Shimon was confident that he had done the right thing in the eyes of *Hashem* and replied with self-assurance, "Do as you see fit!"

The mother and child were sent to the emperor. The trip was a long one. They had not reached their destination by evening and the woman decided to stop for the night and continue on the morrow.

Rabban Shimon's wife was acquainted with a local Roman family. She knocked at their door, her infant in her arms, and was welcomed.

By coincidence, the woman of the house had also given birth to a son just one week before! She had named the boy Antoninus.

The Roman woman asked, "Why have you come this long way with so tender an infant? Could you not have postponed your trip for another time when you and the child are stronger?"

Rabban Shimon's wife heaved a heavy sigh. "Do you think that I am taking a pleasure trip with my newborn?! Certainly not! I must obey the law. Our governor forced me to come to Rome and bring my child before the emperor. I circumcised him against the law and now the emperor must decide my punishment. Who knows what that will be?"

The Roman woman's heart curdled inside her at these words. She was well familiar with the emperor's cruel nature. She had no doubt that he would put her friend and the infant to death without showing any mercy! Suddenly an idea flashed into her head.

"I know! I have found the solution!" she exclaimed. "Tomorrow morning when you continue on your way, you must take my Antoninus and leave your son behind with me. When the emperor sees my uncircumcised son in your arms he will think that someone slandered you falsely. This is the only way to save your life and your infant's life!"

Rabban Shimon's wife accepted the plan. On the following morning she took the little Roman infant in her arms, leaving her own Yehudah behind with her friend.

After a long, arduous journey she finally reached the palace. At the same time the governor of her city had also arrived. He entered the emperor's throne room first to give the background of the case.

"Your Majesty!" he began. "The woman who has just come has violated your law. She and her husband defied you by circumcising their infant son. I have ordered her and her child to appear before you so that you can deal with their treachery yourself."

R' Shimon's wife and her baby were brought in. He immediately ordered the infant seized and examined to see if it was true. The servants took the child and soon reported,

"Your Majesty! The governor is lying! This child is not circumcised!"

"But I am absolutely positive that Rabban Shimon ben Gamliel circumcised his son!" the governor cried out, utterly bewildered. "Surely the G-d of the Jews has performed some miracle here!"

The emperor refused to accept this excuse. He turned to the governor and said sternly, "You sullied the reputation of this innocent Jewess! You accused her falsely! You must be punished. Furthermore, I am hereby revoking the law against circumcision. Let the Jews continue to keep this law as their G-d has commanded."

Rabban Shimon's wife left the palace, bearing the little

Antoninus in her arms. She returned happily to the home of her Roman friend where the exchange of children was made. Antoninus's mother looked at her infant son who had just returned from the king's palace and then said to her friend: "Since *Hashem* saved you and your son through my son, let them forever be friends!"

And so it was. The children grew up: R' Yehudah was appointed as *Nasi* and was revered and loved by his people. Antoninus was chosen as the emperor of Rome. A deep friendship bound the two great men together throughout their lives.

Throughout the reign of Antoninus, the Romans never issued harsh decrees against the Jews. They were free to observe the Torah and its commandments without hindrance.

Some even say that because Antoninus had the privilege of nursing from R' Yehudah's saintly mother — he became worthy of studying Torah from R' Yehudah and eventually, towards the end of his life, actually converted to Judaism!

(According to the *Midrash in Tosafos Avodah Zarah 10b; Menoras Hamaor*)

Buy Cheap Sell Dear

וּבֶן שְׁמֹנַת יָמִים יִמּוֹל לָכֶם כָּל זָכָר

At the age of eight days shall you circumcise to you every male (17:12)

Onkelos, nephew of the Roman emperor Hadrian, desired with all his heart to become a Jew, but greatly feared his powerful uncle.

One day he came to his uncle and said, "I would like to turn my hand to business."

The emperor was surprised and said, "Do you lack money and comforts that you must earn more? My treasure vaults are all open to you!"

Onkelos replied, "But I would like to see the world, to meet different people and to acquire wisdom by experience. Tell me, Uncle, what merchandise should give me a good return?"

Hadrian gave his nephew a piece of advice, "If you see merchandise that has dropped in value — buy it up, for it will eventually rise."

Onkelos sailed for *Eretz Yisrael*. Upon his arrival he went to the Jewish sages and begged them to teach him Torah even before he circumcised himself and became a Jew. But they refused, saying, "The Torah has no lasting effect on someone who is not circumcised."

Onkelos refused to be discouraged. He immediately went and circumcised himself and threw himself bodily into Torah study. He studied and studied incessantly. R' Elazar and R' Yehoshua noticed him one day and saw that he looked different. His face had changed from the vast knowledge which he had acquired. They called him over to them and saw, to their pleasure, that he really understood what he had learned. He was able to ask intelligent questions and give knowledgeable replies.

One day Onkelos decided to return to Rome. Upon his arrival he went to his uncle, the emperor, to pay his respects. His uncle immediately noticed his changed look and asked him what had happened.

Onkelos explained, "This happened because I studied Torah. I also circumcised myself."

"And who advised you to do such a thing?" the emperor asked, surprised.

"You, yourself!" the nephew replied with satisfaction. "Did you not tell me to seek merchandise that was low in value now for it would some day be in great demand? I investigated the religions of all nations and races but could find no people as downtrodden and disgraced as the Jews. I concluded that their day would yet come. Their esteem and value would yet rise to great heights at some future date for it says, 'Thus says *Hashem*, Redeemer of Israel and its Holy One: the despised soul, the abused nation, the servant of rulers will yet see kings, and ministers will rise to bow before it.'"

Hadrian heard these words and became furious. He struck his nephew across the cheek and asked again, "Why did you do it?"

Onkelos confessed, "I wanted to study Torah."

"Why did you not study Torah without circumcising yourself?" the emperor asked.

Onkelos explained, "It is impossible to study Torah without first becoming circumcised for it is written, 'He expounds His words to Yaakov.' Torah can only be taught to one who is circumcised. Yaakov the Patriarch was born circumcised."

He continued, "And in the next verse it says, 'And statutes which are not to be understood' (*Tehillim* 147:19-20). The letters of the word 'bal' — not — hint at the written Torah which begins with the letter 'beis' and ends with a 'lamed'. (*Bereishis* and *l'einei kol Yisrael.*)

(According to the *Midrash Tanchuma Misphatim* 5)

The King's Command

וּבֶן שְׁמֹנַת יָמִים יִמּוֹל לָכֶם כָּל זָכָר

At the age of eight days shall you circumcise to you every
male (17:12)

R' Shimshon Wertheimer was one of the most influential people of the Austrian Empire two hundred years ago. As Economic Minister, he had free access to the palace, to the emperor's ear and to all the state secrets. Being a clever and trustworthy person, he was most highly regarded by King Leopold and, as is always the case when a Jew becomes influential, he had many enemies.

R' Shimshon was an outstanding person, as good as he was rich. A warmhearted person, he never turned away a fellow Jew in distress. His home was open to all the poor and needy of Vienna, to travelers, orphans and widows. His kindness was legendary not only in his city but throughout Europe. Wherever there was a Jewish community faced by harsh decrees or other trouble, its people knew that they had an untiring ally in R' Shimshon. The latter employed his influence at court to help anyone and everyone he could.

R' Shimshon was beloved by his fellow Jews but was also well liked at court. This increased the hatred of his enemies. Among them was a rabid anti-Semitic priest, who plotted and schemed continually of ways to throw R' Shimshon down from his influential post and cast him into disfavor with the emperor.

One time, when he was lucky enough to have the emperor's ear, the priest said belittlingly, "That Jew whom you like so much, Your Majesty, what is his name? Wertheimer? Heh? Well, are you so certain that he is loyal to you? That he only has the country's welfare at heart? I would not be so sure. If I were in your position, Your Majesty, I would not trust him so implicitly..."

"Don't be foolish! He is my right hand! I do not withhold any secrets from R' Shimshon. He is the most honest and trustworthy person I have ever met!"

"Really? And yet I am certain that he is deceiving you!"

The emperor did not react. He trusted R' Shimshon. Still, the latter was a Jew, and you never knew. The priest seized his moment and pressed his point. "I have actual proofs, documents, that the Jew steals from the national treasury. How else do you think he got to be so rich? I bribed one of his private employees to get me copies of his account books. Do you have any idea how rich he actually is?! His wealth is legendary! Why not put him to a test, Your Majesty? Ask him to state the amount of his real wealth. If that sum tallies with the amount on his ledgers, then I will hold my tongue. But if the sum he states is lower than what his books say, then you will know that he is a liar and a thief, that he is stealing from the government, from your own treasury!"

He paused, then spoke in a confidential tone, "And if I am right, Your Majesty, allow me the pleasure of punishing him. Deliver him into my hands; I will know how to take care of the traitor."

"Very well," the emperor agreed, though reluctantly. "I know that you will not find anything amiss in his accounts. Still, if you wish..."

"Do not be so certain, Your Majesty," the priest dared question the emperor's judgment. "I, myself, am so sure of my facts that I want you to order the furnaces heated up already so that he can be thrown in right away. I do not want any delay. He is too clever and slippery..."

The emperor agreed to this too. He sent instructions to his chief executioners to heat the furnaces. After the priest had gone to fetch R' Shimshon — he wanted that satisfaction all for himself — the emperor sent another secret message to the executioners saying: if any high-ranking government official, no matter who, were to later come and ask if the orders had been carried out, they were to seize that person immediately, no questions asked, and throw *him* into the fiery furnace!

With happy heart and light foot the priest left the palace and went to summon R' Shimshon. "I will finally rid myself of this hated man!" he gloated. He could already see in his mind's eye the scorched body of the Jew and the mournful faces of the Jews in Vienna who had used him as their protector.

R' Shimshon went to the emperor at once. He was often summoned at a moment's notice to help him make important diplomatic decisions. The emperor greeted him as warmly as usual and conversed with him at leisure. Then, without forewarning, he sprang his question:

"By the way, R' Shimshon, tell me, how rich are you? What is the extent of your holdings?"

"Thank G-d, I certainly have nothing to complain of, Your Majesty," R' Shimshon replied innocently.

The emperor laughed congenially. "I know that I pay you a very generous salary. I am curious, therefore, to know, at what sum would you estimate your assets? How much are you worth?"

R' Shimshon seemed flustered. "I really could not tell you without first checking my books."

"Oh I don't mean down to the last penny. I mean in general, a broad estimate. How rich would you say you are?"

R' Shimshon made some quick calculations in his head and finally stated a sum that was one tenth of what the priest had said. The emperor seethed with anger but did not show it. So! The Jew had been cheating him all these years! And he had trusted him so implicitly! The priest had been right after all! But he was also grieved. He would be losing a very capable minister, one who had given invaluable advice over the years. He would not have anyone to replace him. Alas! Still, one could not keep such a traitor in one's very palace. With aching heart, the emperor changed the subject and asked R' Shimshon to please do him a service: to go to the chief executioners and ask them if they had fulfilled the royal orders.

R' Shimshon bowed and left the throne room, not suspecting a thing since the emperor's expression or attitude had not visibly changed towards him.

He was about to go to the furnaces at the end of the city when a Jew ran up to him. "You are just the person I have been looking for all morning!" he greeted him breathlessly.

"I have been trying to find a *mohel* for my infant son but have had no luck. Everyone is already busy or out of town. I did not want to disturb you; I know how busy you are with diplomatic affairs, but today is the infant's eighth day. You are my only hope. Surely you cannot refuse me!"

R' Shimshon was an expert *mohel*, among his many

other talents. He never refused the honor of performing a *bris*. And now, especially, when all the other *mohalim* were unavailable, he could not turn down a Jew in need. He followed happily behind the relieved father, intending to perform the emperor's errand later on. He had not said that it was particularly urgent.

Everyone rejoiced to see who the father had finally secured as *mohel* for the infant. The ceremony took place immediately; it was late in the day already. The family insisted that R' Shimshon remain for the *seudas mitzvah* and that he recite the *bircas hamazon* over the cup of wine. When it was all over, R' Shimshon suddenly felt exceptionally tired. He begged for a sofa or bed where he could lie down as he felt weak. The family gave him a quiet room and R' Shimshon fell asleep immediately and slept for many hours.

Meanwhile the priest learned that his plan had gone smoothly. The emperor had questioned R' Shimshon about his wealth and had learned that R' Shimshon had been deceiving him all along. He had sent the Jew to his death and would soon confiscate his property. He exulted. "I must see this with my own eyes!" he said eagerly, impatient to see his enemy dead.

He hurried to the royal furnaces to see if the emperor's orders had been carried out. As soon as he appeared and asked the key question, the executioners did not hesitate but seized him and threw him into the fire. They had expected — and were used to — resistance. But they obediently carried out the emperor's orders.

It was already dark when R' Shimshon awoke. He suddenly remembered that he had forgotten to do the emperor's bidding!

He went home immediately and was greeted by woeful

faces. Meanwhile the emperor's orders had gone into effect and the family had received notice that everything was to be confiscated.

R' Shimshon tried not to worry. As soon as morning dawned he rushed to the royal execution house to ask if the emperor's orders had been carried out.

"Oh, yes," the furnace stokers replied. "We took the priest and above his protests, threw him into the heated ovens. He burned to death."

R' Shimshon was confused but relieved that the emperor's orders had, after all, been carried out satisfactorily despite his delay in relaying the message. He now rushed to report to the emperor that everything was as he desired.

It was now the emperor's turn to be surprised. He looked at R' Shimshon questioningly, as if to ask, "What are you doing here?"

R' Shimshon said, "I must admit the truth, Your Majesty, but I was unable, due to unforeseen circumstances, to carry out your orders right away. But this morning when I went to the executioners, they told me that they seized the priest and threw him into the fire without asking questions, as they had been ordered. And so, everything really turned out as Your Majesty desired."

He then dropped his voice and said shamefacedly, "But, Your Majesty, I would like to know why you ordered my estate confiscated. Have I done anything to displease you? If so, please tell me. All of my fortune has been honestly gained. I can prove it."

The emperor laughed. "You are a very lucky person, R' Shimshon. I see that you must be a worthy one, to have your G-d protect you in such marvelous ways." He then went on to describe what had actually happened and how R' Shimshon had been saved from a terrible death.

He turned to R' Shimshon, saying, "There is still one matter to be cleared up — that of the account books. Can you explain that?"

R' Shimshon then produced his own account books which proved that the priest's had been forged. R' Shimshon was completely exonerated. The emperor felt terrible that he had falsely suspected his most trusted minister.

"What can I do to make amends for my lack of faith in your honesty?" the emperor asked sincerely.

R' Shimshon asked, "You know, Your Majesty, that we Jews are your loyal subjects, that we pray for the welfare of your kingdom. If it pleases you, I would request that you build us a fine synagogue here in Vienna where my countrymen can continue to pray for your success and prosperity. That would be the greatest reward I could possibly dream of!"

The emperor was true to his promise. And before long a magnificent structure graced the city of Vienna, a synagogue known as "R' Shimshon's Synagogue".

A Deep Lesson

אֵין חֵקֶר לִתְבוּנָתוֹ
His discernment is past searching out
(Haftorah Parashas Lech Lecha, Yeshayahu 40)

R' Saadya Gaon, who lived one thousand years ago, was the leader of diasporan Jewry. His name was revered throughout the world, wherever there was a

Jewish community. As head of the great yeshiva in *Bavel*, R' Saadya was forced occasionally to travel abroad but he did not always welcome the fame that accompanied his visits.

One time he came to a certain city and stopped at one of the fine Jewish inns there. The innkeeper noticed the distinguished looking Jew and gave him his best room. He himself tended to the guest's needs, making sure that everything in the room was the finest and the cleanest and that the food was of the highest quality. There was no cause for the guest to complain.

R' Saadya Gaon was unable to keep his identity a secret for long. After a few days it become known that the greatest leader of the generation was in the city. People flocked to pay their respects. When the innkeeper realized who his guest was, he came to him, tears streaming down his cheeks.

"Rabbi, you must forgive me!"

"Forgive you? What wrong did you do?"

"I did not know who you were! Believe me, if I had known that the famous R' Saadya Gaon was staying under my roof, I would have treated you differently."

"But you gave me the very best service possible. I have no cause for complaint. You really outdid yourself!"

"Oh no!" the innkeeper wept. "I didn't realize who you were. Had I known, I would have done much, much more!"

At these words, R' Saadya Gaon himself burst into tears! It was the innkeeper's turn to be surprised. The great man explained:

"I have just learned a very valuable lesson from you! I just learned how much we Jews must honor and respect *Hashem*. We think that we serve *Hashem* properly, that we are able to appreciate Him. But this is ridiculous. With each passing day we see more and more that we cannot grasp even a fraction of His true greatness! What we thought we knew of Him yesterday is less than what we know today. And tomorrow we will be able to appreciate Him more. And yet, all this is still nothing compared to His true greatness which we will never fathom!"

The Magic Earth

יִתֵּן כֶּעָפָר חַרְבּוֹ כְּקַשׁ נִדָּף קַשְׁתּוֹ

His sword makes them as the dust, his bow as the driven stubble (Haftorah Parashas Lech Lecha, Yeshayahu 41)

This pasuk was said regarding Avraham Avinu. In his war with the four kings he would throw earth at them — and it became swords. He would throw straw at them — and it turned to arrows.

(Tractate Taanis 21a)

R'Nachum Ish Gamzu, who lived many many years ago in *Eretz Yisrael*, was an exceptionally wise man. He was called this strange name because he was accustomed to saying the same thing, no matter what happened to him, whether it was good or bad. "*Gam zu letovah* — this, too, is for the best!"

Once, the Jews of *Eretz Yisrael* decided to send a gift to the emperor of Rome who ruled them at that time.

They prepared a beautiful gold casket and filled it up with precious gems and jewels. What a marvelous gift! But who should take it to the emperor?

Unanimously, they decided that Nachum Ish Gamzu was their first choice, the most suitable messenger for such an important mission.

Nachum agreed to undertake this responsibility. He set out for Rome.

Along the way he had to stay overnight in the inn of a gentile. Nachum went to sleep with the casket at his bedside.

The innkeeper had already taken note of the magnificent little chest. It had aroused his curiosity. "What did it contain," he wondered. That night, when Nachum was fast asleep, he crept up to the bedside and very carefully, very stealthily opened it up. He was dazzled by the sight that met his eyes. Even in the dark night, the gems glowed. Unable to contain himself, the innkeeper stole all of the precious gems and replaced them with earth and pebbles.

The next morning Nachum innocently took the casket and continued on his way. He finally reached the emperor's palace.

Ceremoniously, he presented his gift to the emperor. Everyone marveled at the beautiful casket. But when he opened it, he found earth and pebbles.

The emperor flew into a rage and shouted, "The Jews are mocking me! They wish to rebel and this is their way of showing their defiance!" He immediately wrote out a decree of annihilation. All the Jews under his rule were to be destroyed.

Nachum stood there. He did not lose his wits. As usual, he murmured the words that he always said, "This, too,

is for the best."

Hashem saw the great danger which now faced His people and sent Eliyahu Hanavi to save them. Eliyahu came disguised as one of the emperor's ministers and said, "Your Majesty. Do not be angry. Surely this is no ordinary earth. It must have some secret power. Perhaps it is the same type of earth which Avraham their Patriarch used in fighting his enemies. Legend has it that when he threw this magic earth it turned into swords and arrows and won his battle for him!"

The emperor heard this and said, "Very well, let us try it out. Perhaps it is as you say. We have an excellent opportunity, too. The empire has been in the midst of a long, drawn-out war against one rebellious province. Our forces can make no headway. Let us send this earth to the front lines and see if it brings good results."

The earth was sent to the army. The soldiers at the front threw it at the enemy and lo! It turned into spears and swords which found their mark. The enemy was terrified of this new type of weapon and surrendered at once.

When the emperor learned of the miraculous victory, he had Nachum brought before him. He led him to his treasurehouse, filled the casket with gold and silver instead of the miraculous earth that he had brought, and sent him home with great honor.

On his return trip, Nachum stopped to sleep at the same inn that he had visited before. He told the innkeeper about the miracle of the earth and how happy the emperor had been.

The wicked innkeeper, who did not believe in miracles, naively thought that all his soil had a special quality. He tore down the inn and filled wagons with that soil. He drove the wagons to Rome and brought them to the emperor and told him that this was the same earth which the Jew, Nachum, had previously brought.

The emperor was happy at first and sent the earth to be tested in a battle. But when he discovered that it was ordinary earth with no miraculous powers, he ordered the innkeeper seized and put to death.

(According to *Tractate Taanis 21a*)

The Find

אִישׁ אֶת רֵעֵהוּ יַעְזֹרוּ

Each man helps his friend
(Haftorah Parashas Lech Lecha, Yeshayahu 41)

R'Shimon bar Abba was one of the many Sages of *Bavel* who immigrated to *Eretz Yisrael*. He was extremely wise and knowledgeable — and also very poor. Often he did not have anything to eat in his house! Yet, despite his poverty, he never asked for charity and would not even accept it when offered.

The Sages of his city were well aware of how poor R' Shimon was and wished to help him. But they knew that they must do it in a special way. He must not know that the help came from them. Should he discover that they had given money, he would refuse to accept it.

Once, one of the wise men, R' Elazar, had a golden opportunity. One day while walking along the street, he noticed R' Shimon walking a short distance behind him. As usual, R' Shimon was deeply engrossed in his thoughts — Torah thoughts. His head was bowed and his eyes were fixed on the ground.

What did R' Elazar do? He dropped a golden *dinar* and pretended not to know that it has fallen. He then continued on his way without looking back to see what happened. He wanted R' Shimon, who was walking right behind him, his eyes on the ground, to find the money and keep it. A person had every right to keep money found on public property!

R' Elazar hurried away lest R' Shimon discover the trick. But, suddenly, he heard a voice behind him crying, "R' Elazar! Wait a minute, R' Elazar!"

R' Elazar turned his head and saw R' Shimon running towards him. "Look! Look what I found!" he exclaimed, still panting. "This must be yours for you were walking right in front of me." And he tried to give R' Elazar the *dinar*.

"Why do you think that it's mine?" asked R' Elazar. "Lots of people have walked along this road today. One of them must have lost it. But since it is a coin without any identifying marks, it need not be returned. Surely the person who lost it has given up all hope of finding it again! That is the law, you know!"

R' Shimon was forced to agree and kept the money. R' Elazar was overjoyed that his plan had succeeded; he had been able to help the poor R' Shimon.

(According to *Yerushalmi, Bava Metzia Chapter II, Halachah 3*)

A Successful Businessman

אִישׁ אֶת רֵעֵהוּ יַעְזֹרוּ וּלְאָחִיו יֹאמַר חֲזָק

Each man helps his friend and to his brother he says, 'Be strong' (Haftorah Parashas Lech Lecha, Yeshayahu 41)

A blind bagel peddler was sitting on the curb outside the home of R' Yeshaya of Prague, when suddenly a policeman came by and confiscated his entire basket of bagels.

"What shall I do?" the beggar wept. "How shall I earn a living? How can I return home empty-handed?"

R' Yeshaya happened to overhear his weeping and rushed out. "How much were the contents of your basket worth?" he asked kindly.

"Ten rubles!" the man wept, realizing his great loss all over again.

R' Yeshaya took out a ten ruble note and gave it to him.

The blind man showered blessings upon R' Yeshaya's head.

The next day R' Yeshaya waited for the blind peddler to come. As soon as he appeared, he bought his entire stock of bagels, paying him a ten ruble note. Day after day, he would wait for the peddler and buy the whole basket of bagels.

When R' Yeshaya's family noticed this, they were surprised. "Why can't you give him a monthly sum instead of waiting for him, day after day, and buying up his stock. Would it not be much easier both for you and for him?"

"Perhaps. But that is not the point at all! The blind peddler thinks that he is a good businessman and that I buy his bagels because they are so good. This way he feels he is earning a respectable living. Isn't it difficult enough for him being blind? Why should I rob him of the only satisfaction he has in life?"

The Counterfeit Miracle

הֵן יֵבֹשׁוּ וְיִכָּלְמוּ כֹּל הַנֶּחֱרִים בָּךְ

*Behold, all those who were incensed against you shall be
ashamed and confounded*
(Haftorah Parashas Lech Lecha, Yeshayahu 41)

In Damascus over two hundred and fifty years ago there lived a Moslem *fakir* or fanatic who despised and envied the Jews in his city. The *fakir*, an arrogant person, used to boast that each Friday, the holy day of the Arabs, he would fly to Mecca, the holy city of the Arabs, and back. This, was a miraculous feat since Mecca is in Saudi Arabia while Damascus lies in Syria, hundreds of miles away! He hoped to gain more respect by such a tale.

Once time when this *fakir* was out walking, he saw some Jewish children playing merrily. They did not stop their game to bow before him and wish him a good day and he was angered. At once he went to the governor and reported that children had mocked him and the Moslem religion.

The governor immediately ordered the children seized and put behind bars. When the distraught parents learned of this, they went to their great leader, R' Chaim Parchi, one of the members of the Parchi family who were well known throughout Syria as shrewd businessmen, bankers and men of influence in government circles. Besides, they were also learned men, men of Torah and charity. The Parchi home was one of hospitality and scholarship. If anyone could gain the release of the poor innocent children, it would be R' Chaim Parchi.

R' Chaim thought for a moment and hit upon a marvelous scheme. He reassured the worried parents that with the help of *Hashem*, he would outwit the *fakir* and have their children released soon.

R' Chaim owned a vast collection of many valuable pieces of jewelry. One of these was a magnificent necklace made up of ninety-nine perfect gems. Moslem Arabs are accustomed to finger strings of beads, while praying, to keep track of their prayers. Their strings also holds ninety-nine beads.

R' Chaim removed one of the sparkling gems from the beautiful string necklace and headed for the governor's house. He knew that at this particular time he would also find the *fakir* there.

"Your Excellency, I have brought you a gift!' he said, bowing respectfully before the governor.

The governor glowed with pleasure. What a perfect string of precious stones. He held it up to the light. It glowed and shimmered, casting shadows of brilliant color all around the room. Never had he beheld anything so splendid. It would be the envy of all his friends when he went to the mosque to pray. He began fingering the gems when suddenly his face fell. There was one bead missing. There were only ninety-eight. Now he could not use it for his prayers... And he could not flaunt it before his friends... It no longer had any use, any appeal to him, despite the flawless beauty of the ninety-eight precious stones!

Then he had an idea. "Perhaps you can find a matching stone," he said, brightening up.

This is what R' Chaim had been waiting for. "Your Excellency, this string of beads is very rare. I don't think their like can be found in all of Damascus. But in Mecca, I have heard, there is one such gem. Perhaps, when the *fakir* flies to Mecca this Friday," he said innocently, bowing to the other man, "he can fetch it for you. Then your necklace will be complete!"

The governor was overjoyed with the brilliant idea and turned to the *fakir*, his request mirrored on his face.

The *fakir* was in a dilemma. His boast was being challenged and he knew that he could not live up to his words. He had not been to Mecca for years! What could he do? He decided to turn to R' Chaim for help.

This is exactly what R' Chaim had expected. When he came, R' Chaim said, "If you can influence the governor to release the children, I will give you the missing stone, which is in my possession. Then your secret will not be revealed."

They struck a bargain. The children were freed; the governor got his ninety-ninth stone and the *fakir* was not exposed.

פָּרָשַׁת וַיֵּרָא

Parashas Vayeira

The Difference

וַיַּרְא וְהִנֵּה שְׁלֹשָׁה אֲנָשִׁים נִצָּבִים עָלָיו וַיַּרְא וַיָּרָץ לִקְרָאתָם

And he saw and lo! there were three men standing by him.
And he saw and he ran towards them (18:2)

R' Levi Yitzchak of Berditchov, once visited Lvov incognito. He first went to one of the wealthy men of the community, a man who held a prominent position in the city.

R' Levi Yitzchak was dressed simply and looked like a poor man. He was told to wait until the master finished some business and had time to speak to him. Finally, after a long wait, the visitor was ushered into the rich man's presence.

"Might I stay here just until tomorrow?" he asked.

"What?!" the man shouted angrily. "Is that what you came here to ask? What do you think this is, a hotel, an open house? Sorry. Go find a different fool who will let you lounge around in his house."

R' Levi Yitzchak did not reply. He left the house and went to the poor *melamed* to ask for a night's lodging. The latter, who lived in a two room cottage with his large family, did not hesitate, but gladly welcomed the traveler without knowing who he was.

Later that day, when R' Levi Yitzchak went outside, he happened to meet an acquaintance. The latter was surprised to see the great man, but overjoyed that he had decided to grace their city with his presence. Soon he had broadcast the news of R' Levi Yitzchak's arrival all over town and people came flocking to the poor *melamed*'s home to pay their respects. Among the arrivals was the rich man who had previously refused to have R' Levi Yitzchak in his home. He had come to ask the Rebbe's forgiveness for his rude behavior.

"I didn't know who you were. But now that I know that you are the great R' Levi Yitzchak, I beg of you, please come and be my guest. All visiting rabbis are my guests. I have the best accommodations!"

This was not at all the kind of apology that R' Levi Yitzchak wanted. He cared nothing about his own honor but he did resent the rich man's attitude towards hospitality. One did not only offer hospitality to famous people; it should be offered to everyone. And so R' Levi Yitzchak turned to the large crowd of people present and said, "Do you know the difference between Avraham Avinu and Lot, his nephew? Did they not both practice hospitality? Lot also prepared a fine meal, and baked *matzos* for his guests."

The audience looked expectantly and waited for the answer.

R' Levi Yitzchak continued, "By Lot it is written, 'And the angels arrived in Sodom' whereas by Avraham it is written, 'And he saw and lo, three men were standing...' Lot did not see strange *men*, he saw *angels*. Who would not welcome angels into his house?! But Avraham only saw *men*, dusty travelers, hungry and thirsty wanderers, common Arabs. Nevertheless, he still rushed forward to welcome them into his home.

Our Sages say: 'Perhaps you think that the travelers appeared to Avraham as angels?' The answer is no; they looked like common Arabs. Yet, he greeted them warmly. Thus we, the descendants of Avraham, should follow this example and greet people with eager hospitality. I was given this kind of a warm welcome at the home of this humble but pious *melamed*. Is there any reason for me to change my lodgings?"

A Simple Jew

וַיַּרְא וְהִנֵּה שְׁלֹשָׁה אֲנָשִׁים נִצָּבִים עָלָיו וַיַּרְא וַיָּרָץ לִקְרָאתָם

And he saw and lo! there were three men standing by him.
And he saw and he ran towards them (18:2)

R'Shmelke, famous and celebrated throughout Europe, did not enjoy the attention that went with his reputation. He was humble and, thinking himself to be no better than his fellow man, did not want to be treated differently. Thus, when R' Shmelke left Selish to accept the rabbinical position in Balkan, in order to avoid the grand reception that he knew the townspeople were preparing for him, he came a day early.

R' Shmelke checked in at a local hotel without giving

his name. The innkeeper saw a simple man before him and treated him casually, even disparagingly. R' Shmelke did not say a word.

That *Shabbos*, when everyone gathered in the synagogue to hear the new rabbi deliver his sermon, the innkeeper suddenly recognized his guest and was shocked. How he had mistreated him! How shamefully he had behaved! As soon as the sermon was over he rushed to the rabbi to beg his forgiveness.

"I had no idea who you were! Had I known, I would certainly have treated you differently."

"Oh really? I thought that you did know that I was the new rabbi. After all, I am really no one special. But if you did not know who I was and treated me shamefully, thinking me a common Jew, you still did wrong. Why did you not treat me better? Does a simple Jew not deserve decent treatment?"

The Father is Also Cured

וַיַּרְא וְהִנֵּה שְׁלֹשָׁה אֲנָשִׁים נִצָּבִים עָלָיו וַיַּרְא וַיָּרָץ לִקְרָאתָם

And he saw and lo! there were three men standing by him.
And he saw and he ran towards them (18:2)

Our Sages said (as Rashi quotes in Bereishis 18:33): these three men were Michael, Gavriel and Refael. Michael came to bring the tidings to Sarah. Refael came to heal Avraham. Gavriel came to overturn Sodom.

Two infants had been born on the same day in Brody and both of them were to be circumcised on the eighth day. The first *bris* took place immediately after the early dawn prayers. R' Avraham, the Maggid of Trisk, was the *sandak*.

The second *bris* was being delayed. The infant's father lay on his deathbed and the custom in such a tragic situation had always been to postpone the *bris* until the father died so that the infant could bear his name. And so the family waited.

R' Shlomo Kluger, rabbi of Brody, had been invited to serve as the *sandak* of this child. When he learned that the family was waiting for the father to die, he was horrified. He went quickly to R' Avraham and urged that he come with him quickly. They went to the home of the dying man; they found him lying with his eyes tightly shut, his breathing very labored. A *minyan* of men stood around with candles lit, waiting for the soul to depart.

"Stop this! Extinguish those candles at once. We are about to perform a *bris*!" R' Shlomo commanded. At the word '*bris*' the father's eyelids fluttered. R' Shlomo began the ceremony. Suddenly the father's eyes flew open and he asked for some water to wash his hands. After he had washed them, he said that he would like to recite the traditional father's blessing, "...to enter him into the covenant of Avraham Avinu." The ceremony was concluded with great rejoicing.

In the following days the father grew better and better until he recuperated completely and lived for many years.

When R' Shlomo Kluger left the house with the guest, R' Avraham of Trisk, he said, "Do not think for a moment that I have just performed a miracle in bringing about the father's amazing recovery. Not at all. I applied what I learned from the words of our Sages regarding the three angels who visited Avraham. They say that one came to heal Avraham, another to destroy Sodom and a third to inform Sarah of the good news of the future birth of Yitzchak; the third one was also to rescue Lot. 'Why,' thought I, 'was it necessary to send one angel to perform these two tasks? Is there a shortage of angels in heaven?!' The answer is that Lot's merit alone would not have been enough to summon an angel down from heaven. But since he had already come to tell Sarah the good tidings, he was able to save Lot as well.

"Here, too, perhaps, the father's merit alone may not have been enough to warrant a special angel coming to cure him. But when we began the *bris* ceremony, the Angel of the Covenant — Eliyahu Hanavi, came, as he always comes. And once he was here already, he was able to cure the father. And as you see, honored Maggid, my reasoning was correct!"

Thanks to the Mud

יֻקַּח נָא מְעַט מַיִם וְרַחֲצוּ רַגְלֵיכֶם

Let some water be taken and wash your feet (18:4)

The isolated village wore a holiday air. R' Yisrael of Ruzhin was passing through and had decided to remain overnight. The village throbbed with excitement. It was not every day that a great person came to visit the little town.

Before R' Yisrael's coach entered the village, it had

already been decided that Reb Meir, an upright Jew of means who was also well versed in Torah would have the honor of being the Rebbe's host. Reb Meir was a person who gave charity lavishly and it was only fitting that he be allowed this great privilege.

Frantic last minute preparations were being made in Reb Meir's home. The brass door knocker and handle were polished to a brilliant sheen. All the mahogany furniture was polished to bring out the rich hues. Ceilings were swept of cobwebs; floors were waxed; the silver was polished to gleaming brightness; carpets were brushed up. The servants put on clean uniforms and freshly cut flowers were put in crystal vases throughout. The house looked its very finest. Everything was ready for the *tzaddik's* arrival.

The grand coach drove up the swept driveway and the Rebbe was shown to his room. Everything was really sparkling. R' Yisrael nodded in appreciation of all the pains that had been taken for him. He settled in his room to relax after the tiring journey.

The room was comfortably heated, despite the raging cold outside. It was a stormy winter's day. Sleet had fallen, muddying the streets. But inside everything was clean and cozy.

R' Yisrael ate, and drank some tea. By now the townspeople had gathered in front of the house. This was a historic occasion. Everyone wished to take full advantage of it. This would be something to tell grandchildren and great-grandchildren in years to come. Everyone wanted a blessing from R' Yisrael!

The crowds gathered outside. Who had ever realized that so many people lived in this tiny village? Everyone was there — men, women, children and even infants. At first they waited patiently in the freezing weather, oblivious to the wind, cold and sleet. But then they got restless. A few bold ones began pounding on the door. Finally the servant opened the door a tiny bit, expecting to admit people one by one. But seeing their opportunity, the entire group stormed right into the warm house.

Chairs were overturned. Creamy carpets were muddied; crystal vases smashed, paintings thrown to the floor and trodden underfoot. Children climbed up on sofas and armchairs with their muddy shoes and runny noses. Within minutes the lovely home was in shambles. Not that any of the damage was malicious. It just happened.

Reb Meir and his wife stood by, helplessly looking at their beautiful home being irreparably wrecked. A fortune had gone into collecting the beautiful antique furniture and bric-a-brac, into the expensive draperies, and the chandeliers. "What have you done to my beautiful home?" wept Reb Meir.

People looked around and suddenly realized the extent of the damage. They tried to scrape off the mud but it was futile. Reb Meir's home was wrecked. Ruined.

The next few hours were torturous. But by evening the last of the chasidim had finally gone and Reb Meir was left — with whatever was left. Everyone in the village felt good, having had a personal blessing from the *gadol hador*, R' Yisrael of Ruzhin. Reb Meir was too numb to feel anything.

When the last of the stragglers were gone, R' Yisrael called for his host. Reb Meir walked in a daze, past his loyal servants who were trying to bring back a semblance of normalcy to the once beautiful home. He entered R' Yisrael's room, the only one that had been spared the disaster. The Rebbe motioned him to sit down and said,

"Let me tell you a story:

There was once a villager who had six children. His elderly parents also lived with him. Their home was a small shack, not fit to live in. In the winter the roof leaked and the wind whistled through the chinks and cracks. In the summer the hot sun beat down and was unbearable.

It was a particularly stormy winter night. The roof leaked worse than ever. The family huddled under rags, trying to keep warm and dry, which was almost impossible. The hut was dark; they did not even have money for candles, to say nothing of firewood.

The father was curled up in a corner under a ragged, moth eaten coat. He looked around at his family and tears formed in his eyes. "How much longer can we go on like this?" he wondered. "It hurts me to see my wife and children thus. But it hurts me even more to see my poor parents suffering like this in their old age. I should be providing far better for them.'

The fierce storm had broken by morning and the sun was shining again. The father decided that he must make a fresh start. He would seek his fortune in the big city. Things could not get worse than this; perhaps they would get better, he thought optimistically. He took his few rags in a sack and bade his family good-bye.

He trudged along the road for many days, almost starving. He finally reached the big city. But where was he to go? Whom did he know here? He headed for the synagogue, threw himself on a bench, and put his head between his hands. Where would his salvation come from? Who said that life would be any easier here, in the city? Thoroughly discouraged, he wept bitterly, his lips forming a silent prayer.

When he had finished crying, he looked up and noticed someone watching him. "Why are you weeping?" the man asked. "What is troubling you?" The villager poured out his heart to him, describing the condition in which he had left his wife, children and elderly parents. The stranger seemed sympathetic but was not a wealthy person.

"Here," he said. "This is all I can give you. But perhaps you can buy some merchandise with this and get started. It is still better than nothing." He gave the man three coins. "Before you go out to try your luck, come home with me first and let me give you a warm meal. Take a good rest and later you can start on a fresh footing."

After the man had eaten and rested, his host accompanied him to the market. There they were able to buy wares which the man soon sold for a profit of three coins. He turned to his benefactor, wishing to return the coins he had given him but the man said, "You are not yet rich. I do not need the money back now. Wait until you are really prosperous."

The man had six coins in his pocket. Enough to buy food for his family. He decided to return home and not keep them waiting any longer. He went to the market to buy flour, beans, firewood and other basic provisions. When his kind host saw him laden down with packages he offered the loan of his horse and wagon. "When you return next time you can bring them back," he said kindly.

The poor man put his things in the wagon and began traveling home. It was bitterly cold. A strong wind rocked the wagon back and forth. The road was slippery and stony and marked with potholes. The man sat on the driver's seat, praying that he arrive home safely.

But luck was against him. Suddenly the horse stumbled

against a rock and fell into a muddy hole, overturning the wagon. All of the bundles fell into the snow and mud, scattering far and wide. The poor man himself was thrown and suffered several bruises. He lay on the ground. This was the final stroke of ill luck. Even his borrowed horse and wagon had suffered damage. What should he do now?! But he did not succumb to despair. Slowly, he picked himself up and began gathering his possessions. He tried to help the horse out of the pit and to right the wagon. But he did not have the strength to do so. Again and again he failed to budge the vehicle. Snowflakes began drifting down. They soon fell faster and faster. The poor man sat down upon one of the bundles and burst into bitter tears.

Just when everything seemed lost, a carriage came into view. It belonged to a rich man who was traveling by. Despite the shrieking of the wind, he heard the sound of sobbing and told his driver to stop and see what was the matter. He, too, got out of his warm carriage to see what had happened. Immediately they set their shoulders to the task and soon the wagon was back on its wheels and the horse ready to go. They gathered up the bundles, tied them securely and loaded them back on to the wagon. The poor man looked on speechless. He finally uttered his fervent thanks. But that was not the end of the story. The rich man took the poor man into his own coach, gave him a warm drink from a flask and some nourishing food. He told his driver to tie the wagon behind the coach and to drive quickly. After several hours, he delivered the poor man to his very doorstep and even helped him unload his bundles and bring them in.

When the wealthy traveler entered the rickety shack, he was shocked. He had not realized that people could live like that! As soon a they saw their father, the children jumped upon him, begging him for food. The rich man's heart was torn by the pitiful sight. He took out a purse containing six hundred gold coins and gave it to the poor man.

"Here, take this. Buy yourselves some food first. Then get yourself suitable lodgings. This house is not fit for human beings! Afterwards, take the remaining money and open a business so that you can support your family."

The man tried to thank his benefactor but the rich man would not hear of it. He left the shack as soon as he could, thanking *Hashem* in his heart for having given him the opportunity to do such a good deed, to save an entire family. He continued on his way with great joy.

Many years passed and the rich man died. He came before the heavenly court. 'Did you conduct your affairs honestly?" he was asked. Before he could answer, hundreds of evil angels came to seize him. The heavenly court sentenced him to *gehennom*.

But before the avenging angels could lead him away, another angel stepped forward, saying, 'How can a man who saved many lives be sent to *gehennom*? Do the Sages not say that whoever saves even one life is credited with having saved an entire world?'

The angel demanded a retrial. The heavenly court decided to weigh all of the man's deeds again: his sins on one side of the scale and his good deeds on the other. The defending angel placed the poor man, his six children and his parents on the scale. But the good deeds did not outweigh the man's sins.

'What about the wagon?' asked the rich man's defending angel. 'My client helped pull it out of the mud and then he had it towed all the way to the poor man's house. By rights, the wagon should also go on the scale.' The horse and wagon were placed on the heavenly scale. And still the good deeds did not outweigh the sins.

But the defense would not rest yet. The angel fetched all of the mud and dirt that had stuck to the wagon wheels, to the horse, and to the bundles, and heaped that onto the scale. The scale began tipping; the good deeds outweighed the sins.

R' Yisrael had finished his tale. Reb Meir lowered his glance as R' Yisrael spoke once more, "Did you hear that, Reb Meir? Sometimes even the mud on Jewish feet can save a person from *gehennom*. So why are you complaining?"

A Favorable Time

בְּעֵת חַיָּה וְהִנֵּה בֵן לְשָׂרָה
At this season Sarah will have a son (18:10)

Many chasidim came year after year to be with R' Yosele of Reshkov at the *Pesach seder*. It was a time of joy, of spiritual elevation. This was not so for one chasid and his wife. They, too, spent each *Pesach* with the Rebbe, but they came to him in sad spirits and left just as unhappy as they had come.

This couple had not been blessed with children. Year

after year they begged the Rebbe to pray for them but each time he would say, "It is not yet time."

And so it happened again this particular year. The childless couple had come to the Rebbe begging that he pray for them. But he just shook his head sadly, saying, "The time is not yet ripe..."

That night was the first *seder* night. All the chasidim gathered at the Rebbe's table, the few women who had come stayed behind the curtain separating them from the men. The *seder* was drawing to a close as the Rebbe began to sing the *Shir HaShirim* with deep concentration. The chasidim swayed to the Rebbe's melodious voice. And then they too began to sing of *Hashem*'s longing for His people and of their yearning for the ultimate redemption, the *geulah*. A special mood gripped everyone. And when the Rebbe got up to dance, all the chasidim joined hands and formed a circle — all, except the childless chasid. He sat in a corner, forlorn. How could he rejoice if the Rebbe had again rejected his plea? He looked towards the women's section and saw his wife standing there, troubled, in tears.

The Rebbe danced as if he were in another world. But when he had finished and wished to return to his seat, he found his way barred by the childless woman.

"Rebbe! You must help me! I swear that I will not move from here until you promise me children!" she insisted. Then realizing what she had done, she was horrified, for the Rebbe fixed her with his piercing look. She was about to retreat, when, suddenly she heard the Rebbe raising his voice. But he was not speaking to her. His gaze was fixed upward and then he spoke:

"In the *Mishnah* in *Pesachim* it says: 'the first cup of wine is poured and here the son asks.' But I ask You,

Master of the world! How can the son ask, if there is no son? Why do You not grant this childless couple a son to ask the Four Questions? And our Sages further said: 'it is a custom to distribute nuts and almonds to the children on the night of *Pesach* so that they will not fall asleep and will ask the questions.' But I ask You, *Hashem*. To whom can this couple give nuts and almonds? Why should You not give them children so that they can fulfill this holy Jewish custom too?"

R' Yosele was silent. Then he looked at his chasidim and said, "Do you know that *Pesach* is a favorable time for the barren to be blessed with children? Sarah Imenu, who was also childless, was blessed on *Pesach* for that is when the angels came to tell her that at the same time the following year she would bear Yitzchak."

He now turned to the woman who was still standing in his way and said kindly, "Yes, *Pesach* is a favorable time for the barren to be blessed. And now, go back to your place. I hereby bless you that at this same time next year you will be embracing a child."

And indeed, the *tzaddik's* blessing came true.

Paying for an Insult

אֲשֶׁר יְצַוֶּה אֶת בָּנָיו... לַעֲשׂוֹת צְדָקָה וּמִשְׁפָּט

That he will command his sons... to do charity and justice
(18:19)

When it came to his own family, R' Chaim of Sanz lived very frugally, pinching every penny, living in poverty. But when someone else was concerned, R'

Chaim was lavish. Hundreds, if not thousands, of people were aided by the charity which he gave unstintingly. R' Chaim used to collect *tzedakah* from the people of Sanz and from all the chasidim who came to him for a *brachah*, but would immediately distribute this money to the poor. He was especially concerned with *hachnasas kallah*, marrying off poor or orphaned young girls and youths. He toiled tirelessly until he had the sum to provide them with new clothing, dowry and all wedding expenses. Then, when he was invited to the weddings of the people he had helped, he would rejoice as if they were his own children!

One time R' Chaim was sitting together with his son, R' Yechezkel of Shinova, and another rabbi from a nearby town. They were discussing a Torah topic when suddenly there was a knock at the door.

The local *melamed* entered the room, his shoulders bowed.

"And when will we be able to dance at your daughter's wedding?" the Rebbe asked heartily, knowing that the *melamed's* daughter was engaged to be married.

The man shrugged his shoulders, as if to say that he did not know.

The Sanzer Rebbe looked alarmed. "What is the matter? Why can't you set a date for the wedding?"

"I cannot afford a new *tallis* and *shtreimel* for the *chasan* as is customary," he said unhappily.

"But father," R' Yechezkel whispered loudly enough for everyone to hear, "I just saw him buying a *tallis* and *shtreimel* the other day!"

Confused and embarrassed, the *melamed* rushed out of

the room. He had hoped to ask the Rebbe to help him out but now...

The Rebbe turned to his son and scolded him, "Now look at what you have done! You embarrassed a Jew! Why did you jump to conclusions? Perhaps he ordered a *tallis* and *shtreimel* but did not have the money to pay for them; perhaps he needs a new dress for his wife for the wedding but is too ashamed to ask for it and therefore was going to ask money for the other things? How did you have the arrogance to shame a person publicly?! How will you defend yourself when you stand before the heavenly court? What will you say?"

R' Yechezkel accepted his father's reproof and rushed outside to overtake the *melamed* and ask his forgiveness. When he caught up with him, the latter seemed more embarrassed than ever.

"Please forgive me!" R' Yechezkel begged. The man shook his head. He had been deeply hurt and said: "I want you to come back with me to the Rebbe. I want to have a proper *din Torah* with you. Only then will I forgive you."

The two walked back silently together. When they stood before R' Chaim, his son, R' Yechezkel, apologized sincerely once again. But before the *melamed* could accept the apology, the Rebbe spoke up:

"I don't think that you should forgive him at all now! First make sure that my son promises to buy you a *shtreimel* and a *tallis* and to collect the entire sum for the wedding expenses."

R' Yechezkel agreed. Only then did the Sanzer Rebbe allow the *melamed* to accept his apology and forgive him.

Before Whom You Stand

וְאַבְרָהָם עוֹדֶנּוּ עֹמֵד לִפְנֵי ה׳

And Avraham was still standing before Hashem (18:22)

B y the side of the highway stood a Jew, praying. His
eyes were on his *siddur*; but his heart was directed
towards heaven. He uttered each word with a sweetness
and fervor, concentrating upon each thought. It was
evident just by looking at him that he fully knew before
Whom he was standing in prayer! This was no common
person, but a holy man.

Suddenly, footsteps could be heard. A stranger was
approaching. But the good man paid no attention to the
footsteps. Not for one instant did he tear his attention
away from his prayer or his *siddur*.

A few minutes passed and the stranger was now
standing right by the side of the praying Jew. He looked
at the Jew in astonishment. How could he be so
indifferent to what was going on about him? Was he not
curious to see who was standing at his side? Or was he
perhaps deaf and dumb?

And who was this stranger, gazing in amazement at
the praying Jew?

He was a high-ranking Roman officer, a man of power,
a man whom people feared.

The officer stood in front of the Jew and greeted him.
He was certain that now the praying man would turn to

him and return his greeting. But he was disappointed. The Jew did not react at all. He continued nodding back and forth, whispering to himself, paying absolutely no attention to the officer who had been standing by his side for several minutes now.

The officer took this as a personal offense. He was deeply insulted. His face turned red with rage. He began pacing back and forth in front of the praying man, muttering angry words under his breath.

Still the Jew did not react. He behaved as if nothing at all had happened and went on praying as before, with the same fervor.

The officer waited with suppressed fury. The *tzaddik* finished his prayers, took the three steps backwards, murmured some words, then took three steps forward. Then, only then, when he had finished praying, did the Jew turn his attention to the officer standing in front of him.

The *tzaddik's* quiet, peaceful glance met the fiery, glowering look of the officer.

"You fool!" thundered the officer. "Why didn't you return my greeting? Have you no fear of a Roman officer? If I so desired, I could cut off your head here and now. No one would save you!"

The officer shouted with all his might but the Jew just stood there, calmly and quietly, not at all intimidated by the threats. He waited until the officer had finished his tirade, then began to speak gently, "Please, do not be upset, honored officer! Wait a minute while I explain."

The officer remained silent and waited with curiosity to hear the Jew explain his strange behavior.

The Jew began with a question. "If you were standing before your emperor and a friend came along and greeted you, would you return his greeting?"

The officer expressed astonishment at the unusual question. He could not understand how it related to the matter at hand. Nevertheless, he hastened to reply, "What a question?! I would not dream of doing such a thing!"

"And let us say that you did return his greeting. What would happen to you in such a case?"

"I would have my head handed to me for such a breach of courtesy."

"Fine! Then just think of what you yourself have just said!" the Jew replied, raising his voice with confidence. "Your emperor before whom you were theoretically standing, is a king of flesh and blood, a mortal who will rule for some time and then die, like all men. What will his power be then? And still, you tremble before him and would not speak to anyone else while standing in his presence. As for me — I was standing before the King of kings, Who lives and rules forever. Should I not tremble in His presence? Would I have been justified in interrupting my prayer to Him and speaking to you?"

The Jew's words made a deep impression upon the Roman officer. He forgave him and allowed him to continue on his journey.

(According to Tractate *Berachos* 32*b*)

The Innocent Sheep

חָלִילָה לְּךָ... וְהָיָה כַּצַדִּיק כָּרָשָׁע

Far be it from you... and the righteous will be like the sinner
(18:25)

I t was not an uncommon sight for a Jew to enter a strange *beis medrash* and ask for help to marry off his daughter. Before a girl got married, her father had to provide her with a decent dowry and he also had to pay for the wedding expenses. People who worked hard for a living and could barely make ends meet, could barely feed and clothe their families, were very hard put to marry off their children. But no one would even consider a match before some promise was made on both sides. And when desperate fathers could not come up with the necessary funds, they would be forced to go from city to city in the hope of gathering the sum to make the wedding possible.

This was the plight of the poor man who entered the *beis medrash* in Pshischa one morning, begging for help. He looked more desperate than most beggars and after speaking to him, one particular young man's heart went out to him. "I want to help you very much," he said, "but it will take a few days until I can make the rounds of the rich people here. Can you stay here for that time?"

The man shook his head. He still had many other cities to visit. And his family was waiting for him at home, trying to make preparations for the wedding — without any money. "I can only remain here today," he said sadly.

The young man thought hard, then made his decision.

"I am responsible for the fund to repair all the *siddurim* and study books here. I will borrow money from this fund, since there are no pressing needs, and I will make it up over the month by collecting for this man's *hachnasas kallah*."

The young man gave the poor man a decent sum and received a fervent blessing in return. The visitor left to visit the next place of call.

The young man had made no secret of his 'loan'. Many people were sympathetic to what he had done. The community of Pshischa was not a stingy one. R' Simchah Bunim of Pshischa, a close friend of this young man, a study-partner of his group, actually praised him for what he had done. "Helping to marry off a young Jewish girl establishes a home; it is like saving a Jewish life which itself is like saving an entire world! You did the right thing, my friend!"

But not everyone felt so; the young man also had his enemies. There were certain members of that congregation who vehemently opposed his having 'borrowed' from public funds, even for charity. Interestingly, not one of these members was a Torah scholar. Rather, they were unlearned men who never attended even the simplest *shiurim*, yet they voiced their opinions as if they were the *halachic* experts. They held a public hearing and imposed a heavy fine upon the young man. They wished him to serve as an example for all.

R' Simchah Bunim was determined to defend him. But how could he appeal to these people if they did not even speak his language — the language of Torah? How could he explain to them in *halachic* terms that the young man had done the right thing? He had to speak to them on their own level.

Finally he stood up and said: "Gentlemen: I have a difficulty in understanding a verse in *Tehillim*. Perhaps you can help me. King David says: 'I strayed like a lost sheep, seek (Your servant)...' (The word 'seek' appears as *'bakesh'* in the *Tehillim*. R' Simchah Bunim pretended that it read *'bekash'* — straw.) Now I would like to ask you fine people: what does 'the sheep was lost because of straw' mean? Can anyone explain this to me?"

Of course no one knew the answer.

"Very well," continued R' Simchah Bunim. "I will tell you a story. Once, a terrible epidemic erupted in the forest. Animal after animal sickened and died until the king of the beasts, the lion, decided to do something. He ordered every animal to come before him and confess to its sins. The lion appointed a panel of judges to hear the confessions and decide which animal was responsible for the epidemic.

"The first to appear was the tiger. Growling ferociously, he confessed to once having attacked a human being. 'I was starved and when he crossed my path, I could not help pouncing on him. I tore him to shreds and ate him up. This happened many years ago but the deed has been lying on my conscience. Now that we have been ordered to confess, I must admit to my sin.'

"The panel of judges huddled together with the lion to review the case. After much whispering they finally ruled that the tiger was innocent. 'It is his nature to kill. What could he do if he was hungry and could find no other prey? He only did what was natural.'

"The next to appear before the panel was the wolf. He also had a confession to make. 'I know that it is forbidden to slay an animal and its parent on the same day. Still, I could not help myself. I once saw a cow grazing with her young calf. I pounced upon the calf and ate it up but, still, my hunger was not satisfied. I killed and ate the cow as well. I am afraid that I am to blame for the epidemic.'

"The panel retired to discuss the case. They came back with the verdict of 'innocent'. What was a wolf to do if he was hungry? He had no choice but to kill. Was he not called a 'devouring wolf'? No, he only followed his instinct and could not be blamed for that.

"Much relieved, the wolf left the court and, lo and behold, a small sheep arrived. Humbly, its knees knocking with fear and awe, it stood before the lion and the panel of judges. 'I have a confession to make. I am afraid that I am the real cause of the epidemic amongst the animals. This past winter was very cold. Fearing that I might freeze to death, my master took me into his house which was warm. But he forgot to feed me. When my blood began to flow once again I felt terribly hungry, but there was nothing for me to eat. That night, before my master went to bed, he took off his shoes. There, in one shoe, I saw a stalk of straw, just the thing I was longing for. I could not help myself. I ate it,' the sheep confessed with a deep sigh. 'I am to blame for the terrible epidemic. My sin of stealing brought it on.'

"All at once the animals of the forest pounced upon the little sheep. 'Aha!' they shouted. 'Here is the culprit! This is the guilty one! This sheep stole some straw and we must pay for his sin?'

"Now, my friends," concluded R' Simchah Bunim after a brief pause, "you can understand the verse. In this tale only the innocent sheep 'sinned'. Only she was 'guilty' while all the other animals of the forest, who killed and preyed without conscience — were 'innocent'! This is exactly the case here!"

Before the men could open their mouths to defend themselves, R' Simchah Bunim attacked them: "What is your name, Mister. *Volf*, isn't it? Wolf? And you, there? *Ber* or bear. And you on the right, *Aryeh Leib*, lion, am I not correct? Each one of you has a sack full of sins tied around your necks yet you all consider yourselves righteous and worthy enough to judge this poor innocent sheep whose only sin is eating a bit of straw, borrowing communal funds for a worthy purpose, intending to raise it himself. And yet his sin is too great for the community to overlook!"

The men understood the comparison and lowered their eyes in shame. They dropped the 'charges' against the young man and canceled the fine which they had imposed.

On the Way to the Rebbe

כִּי אָמַרְתִּי רַק אֵין יִרְאַת אֱ־לֹהִים בַּמָּקוֹם הַזֶּה וַהֲרָגוּנִי

For I have said, but there is no fear of G-d in this place and they shall kill me (20:11)

When there is no fear of Hashem — one can go as far as
shedding blood.

(Writings)

Reb Moshe was an ardent follower of the great Rebbe Yisrael of Ruzhin but he lived in the isolated Ukraine, in a village near Zitomir and could only visit the

Rebbe twice a year, on *Chanukah* and *Shavuos.*

One year, just before *Chanukah*, Reb Moshe was making his usual pilgrimage when he got caught in a snowstorm. Luckily he was not far from an inn owned by a Jewish innkeeper whom he knew from past years. He was not too upset by the delay, since this innkeeper was also a chasid of R' Yisrael and the two used to spend many happy hours telling over the wonders which the Rebbe had wrought. This time, too, they stayed up until late at night, speaking about the Rebbe's greatness and miracles to a rapt audience of the innkeeper's children.

A short while after everyone had finally gone to sleep, there was a loud pounding on the door. The innkeeper paid no attention since drunken farmers seeking a drink of liquor sometimes tried to get him out of bed. If he ignored them they usually went away.

This time, however, the pounding did not stop. The innkeeper could hear many rowdy voices outside. It sounded like a band of robbers. He debated whether to go down and open up the door lest they batter it down, or stay where he was and hope that they would go away. By the time he decided to give in, the men had already burst through the door. They seized the innkeeper and his family and bound them up. Then, they began drinking to their heart's content.

Reb Moshe, temporarily safe in his own room, knew that soon the bandits would begin a thorough search of the inn and would find him. Chances were that they would not be content with his money, especially since he did not have much with him, and would kill him in their drunkenness. But there was nothing for him to do except pray. Reb Moshe took out a volume of *Zohar* and began reciting from it. He was soon so rapt up in it that he forgot all about the danger threatening him. His voice rose until it could be heard downstairs.

"Who is that reading aloud so confidently?" the leader asked, storming up the stairs to discover the source of the voice.

He burst into the room but suddenly stopped in his tracks. He knew this man! It was Moshe, his childhood friend! They had learned together in the same *cheder*!

Suddenly a flood of nostalgia swept over the robber. Those had been good days, carefree days. What fun he had had playing childish pranks with this same Moshe. Without offering any explanations, he turned back to his companions and said,

"Let's free these people and continue on our way. We have had our fling."

The robbers were astonished but were afraid to question their leader's decision. They began untying the innkeeper and his family.

While they were busy working, the leader entered Reb Moshe's room and began talking to him in a conversational tone.

"*Shalom aleichem*, Reb Moshe. How have you been? What have you been doing with yourself these past years?"

Reb Moshe knew that his life still hung in the balance. Just one false move and he might incur the chief's anger. Still, he had been asked a civil question and so he replied politely, trying to hide his fear. In a few sentences he outlined the happenings of his life.

The leader nodded, then said, "You are probably curious about me too. Let me review my own story. I married the daughter of an innkeeper and moved in with the family. My father-in-law supported us while I pursued my studies. I fit in well with the family; they all liked me.

"One time, while I was engrossed in my study at home, my wife burst into the room and said; 'I have never bothered you before but there is a chance for us to make some money now. It would be nice to have some money of our own and not always be dependent upon my father's handouts. You know how unpleasant it is to ask, even though he does not begrudge us anything. But if you pay attention, you can hear sounds of argument in the tavern. There are a group of gentiles who have made some money in a business deal but do not know how to divide it up fairly. You are good at figures. You are also a respected person, a scholar. I think that they will be very grateful if you untangle their financial affairs and divide their money between them equitably. It should not take up too much of your time. Besides, I am sure that they will pay you generously for your services.'

"Innocently, I entered the tavern room and offered to settle their quarrel. They were all pleased at my fair handling of the argument and paid me for my trouble. About two months later the same thing happened again. I heard sounds of argument coming from the drinking room. Not waiting for my wife to come, I went to the gentiles and again settled their affairs to their satisfaction. They paid me very well. This time, however, my conscience did not rest easy. I could not help overhearing their talk and learned that their money had not been honestly gained. Thus, I felt like a partner, an accomplice to their crime. I told this to my wife but she shrugged my fears away. 'What business is it of yours how they got their money? It is not your affair and you certainly are not to blame.' Her words reassured me.

After that, I was frequently called upon to arbitrate, that is, to divide up the loot. By the time I admitted to myself that I was dealing with a band of thieves, it was already too late. I had incriminated myself. I knew too much. They would not let me out even if I wanted to quit. I was no longer the innocent fellow I had been. I was now a true partner in crime.

"I tried evading them, but each time my wife convinced me that I was only an accountant, only a peace-maker. Had I stolen? Had I robbed?

"I became deeper and deeper embroiled in the affairs of these gentiles until their thefts no longer even bothered my conscience. Meanwhile, we were becoming richer and richer...

"One night I was woken out of a deep sleep by a knock at my window. I saw a familiar face outside and quickly opened the door. It was one of the robbers. He told me that his band was in danger. They had lain in ambush for a nobleman whom they knew had withdrawn a large sum of money from the bank. But he had not been caught by surprise. He was well armed and together with his driver, was holding his own bravely against the robbers. 'If the men are caught, you will be implicated too!' the robber threatened me.

"'Do something!' my wife urged hysterically. I panicked. How could I resist these two people? In desperation, I grabbed a hammer and followed the robber. After a short walk we came upon the struggling men. The battle was still evenly balanced but it looked like the nobleman might win. I sprang upon him from behind and landed a heavy blow with my hammer. It crushed his skull like an eggshell. That blow sealed my fate. Once I had murdered I could not stoop any lower. I joined the group, participated in all of their raids and soon became their leader.

"And that is how you see me tonight, on the job, raiding and robbing as usual." the leader confessed. A tear escaped his eye and dropped to the ground. "Seeing you tonight has brought a drastic change in me. I feel ashamed for everything. I cannot return to such a life of sin. I must escape this band. I don't care what happens to me any more, whether or not I die. But I cannot go back to a life of crime. Just looking at you, reciting those holy words, has transformed me completely."

Reb Moshe tried to comfort him. "Don't say that all is lost. There is always *teshuvah*, repentance. Come with me to the Ruzhiner Rebbe, R' Yisrael. He will set you on the road to *teshuvah*."

Reb Moshe succeeded in convincing his childhood friend and together they slipped away in the night and found their way to R' Yisrael. And the robber chief became in due time a genuine *baal teshuvah*.

Joining in the Mitzvah

וַיִּטַּע אֶשֶׁל

And he planted an 'eishel' (tamarisk tree) (21:33)

R' Elimelech of Lizensk was a beloved and famous Rebbe. Wherever he went he was given a grand welcome and when he left, a honorable leavetaking. Jews everywhere flocked to receive his blessing or, at the least, to gaze at his holy face and be inspired.

One time when R' Elimelech was leaving a city, everyone turned out to see him on his way. R' Elimelech who was riding in his carriage chanced to glance back and saw the crowd of people streaming behind. Suddenly he turned to his driver and asked him to stop the coach. He got out and joined the crowd.

"What is the matter, R' Elimelech?" people asked. "Why did you get out to walk?"

He smiled and answered, "I saw this large group of Jews eagerly performing the important *mitzvah* of seeing off guests, and I, too, wished to, somehow, join in the *mitzvah!*"

The Fire

וַיִּטַּע אֵשֶׁל
And he planted an 'eishel' (tamarisk tree) (21:33)
'Eishel' (alef, shin, lamed) is an abbreviation for achilah,
shesiyah, levayah (food, drink, seeing a guest off)
(Writings)

A villager once burst into the study of the Maggid of Kozhnitz, all upset. A terrible fire had just broken out in his inn, consuming everything that he owned.

"I don't understand it, Rebbe. I have been a G-d fearing

Jew all my life. I keep an inn and run my business honestly. I welcome each guest warmly and feed him well, even if he is a wandering beggar and cannot pay. I am certainly not worse than the next Jew. Why then has this catastrophe happened to me?"

The Rebbe listened while he ranted and raved. Then he replied, "You may have treated your guests properly but hospitality does not end at your doorstep. You must also accompany them a few steps, and see that they have provisions for the road ahead. This is an important part of hospitality; it is the *lamed* of *eishel, levayah*, to escort them. And since you forgot this vital point, all that remained from your *eishel* was *eish* or fire."

The Western Wall

בְּתוֹךְ עַמִּי אָנֹכִי יֹשָׁבֶת

I live in the midst of my people
(Haftorah Parashas Vayeira, Melachim II, 4)

One of R' Moshe Iver's outstanding traits was his humility. Even after he became a famous rabbi, after hundreds sought his advice or came to him with their *halachic* questions, he acted with modesty. Instead of sitting by the respected eastern *mizrach* wall of the synagogue together with the president and the noted scholars, he remained huddled at the opposite side, at the western wall. No amount of persuasion could make him change his place. The congregants were deeply upset, not only for the rabbi's honor but also for the honor of the Torah, and told him so.

R' Moshe nodded his wise head and said, "The western wall is nothing to be ashamed of, my dear friends. In fact, it was only the western wall of the *Beis Hamikdash* which was spared destruction when the rest of the House was razed to the ground. And do you know why? Because it was here that the poor people, the humble folk, huddled together to pray. It was this wall which was dearest to *Hashem*."

Techiyas Hameisim

וַיִּפְקַח הַנַּעַר אֶת עֵינָיו
And the lad opened his eyes
(Haftorah Parashas Vayeira, Melachim II, 4)

Life for the Jews of Jerusalem was not easy under foreign rule. Several hundred years ago, when they were ruled by a non-Jewish governor, the gentile inhabitants of the holy city plotted to bring disaster upon the Jewish community. At first they attempted to slander the Jews in order to make the ruler pass harsh decrees against them. But the governor was not a cruel man and would not pass evil laws without justification. He refused to listen to the villains.

The non-Jews were furious. They now included the ruler in their hatred and sought their revenge against him for not cooperating with them. The best way to strike back at him, they decided, was to murder his only son, the apple of his eye. They plotted to kidnap the boy and kill him. Then they would throw his body into the Jewish section, incriminating the Jews. It was a perfect crime.

The plotters laid their plans carefully. The scheduled day arrived. They laid an ambush for the boy along the road which he took every day and with promises of fine gifts, led him to a secluded spot where they carried out their terrible scheme. The lad cried out for help but there was no one to hear him. The murderers killed him in cold blood and gathered his blood into a jar. Then they waited for night to fall.

It was pitch dark, past midnight, by the time they dared move. The last lanterns and candles had already been extinguished and the streets were completely dark. The perfect cover for a terrible crime. The murderers crept through the Jewish quarter, the boy's body slung over their shoulders. They threw the body into the courtyard of the synagogue, then spilt the blood they had gathered in the jar onto the floor to make it look as if the boy had been murdered on that very spot. The deed done, they slipped away through the silent streets without any witnesses to their shocking crime.

The ruler had been waiting for the return of his son since the afternoon. The boy never dallied; he was a dutiful son. What was keeping him? As the hours passed the father grew more and more worried. After nightfall, he decided to call on the police to make a thorough search. He also issued an order that anyone who had seen the boy should report at once to the governor's mansion. The entire city took part in the search, for the ruler was well liked. They combed the cellars, wells, junk heaps, open fields... Not a trace could be found. Finally, someone suggested that they search the Jewish quarter, in the synagogue courtyard. And there on the floor of the courtyard lay the child, his throat slit, the blood smeared all over the ground around him.

The searchers rushed back to the governor to report their frightful findings and behind them came the police, carrying the lifeless body of the ruler's only son.

"Look at what the Jews did to you!" the non-Jews cried. "This is how they show their loyalty! And yet you favor them! Do you still think them to be such good people?!" The mob became worked up and screamed, "We demand justice! We want blood!"

The governor was beside himself with rage. He could not think straight. He would show the Jews... He summoned the heads of the Jewish community and said:

"One of you did this to my son! I demand that you find the murderer. I want him brought to me by tomorrow. If you cannot produce the guilty man, I will destroy you all!"

The Jews were panic-stricken. "Give us at least three days, Your Excellency. We will do our best." He agreed to wait the three days.

The Jews of Jerusalem gathered in their synagogues and prayed for three days and three nights. But no help was in sight. Finally, when the leaders were summoned before the ruler one holy man, R' Klonimus, offered to go alone. Everyone knew R' Klonimus to be a saintly man who spent his days and nights in prayer and study. Even the non-Jews respected him.

R' Klonimus went to the governor alone. Falling at his

feet, he begged for one more hour in which to pray. "I will soon be able to tell you who the real murderer is. I will be able to prove it too."

The governor nodded. R' Klonimus hurried out of the room and went directly to the synagogue. He stood before the *aron kodesh* and burst into tears. He begged his Father in heaven to help the Jewish community. He knew that his people were innocent. Why were the Jews always the scapegoat for all gentile woes? Why were they always the first to suffer? He begged *Hashem* to have mercy upon them. He recited *Tehillim* and said the Thirteen *Midos* of *Hashem's* mercy. When the hour was over, the governor's guards came to fetch R' Klonimus. The Jews had been given every possible chance, but now they must explain how the body had reached the synagogue courtyard.

R' Klonimus entered the governor's reception chamber. The body of the murdered child was lying in an open oak coffin, embalmed, ready to be buried. The highest officials stood around, waiting for the outcome of this meeting. "How would the Jew defend his community?" they wondered. "Surely now they would see the downfall, of this holy man and his fellow Jews!"

R' Klonimus asked for a piece of paper. He made some markings on it, then placed it upon the forehead of the dead child.

Suddenly, the dead boy stood up!

R' Klonimus then, spoke to him, "My son, I want you to tell all these people exactly how you were murdered."

The boy pointed to the men who had done the terrible deed. They were all in the room, gleefully expecting to see the ax fall upon the Jewish community. But now they turned a deathly white and held their breath while the boy spoke, describing exactly how he had been tricked into following these men, whom he knew through his father. He explained how everything had been planned to make it look as if the crime had taken place near the synagogue.

The men began shivering with fear. And the boy continued, "Don't you believe me, father? Well then, send some soldiers to the empty field right outside the city. There, on a large flat stone you will find some more bloodstains. That is the spot where I was really murdered. Go there and see if it is not true."

A servant was quickly sent to verify the lad's words. He returned and said that it was exactly as the boy had said. The boy then sank back into his coffin, lifeless as before. R' Klonimus removed the paper from his forehead and kept it for it contained a holy Name. The real murderers saw that they could no longer pretend innocence. They threw themselves at the governor's feet, confessing their guilt but pleading for mercy. The governor ordered them seized and thrown into jail, pending trial.

The Jews were cleared of all blame. And from then on, the governor respected them, even more than before, because their G-d had performed such a miracle in order to save them.

פָּרָשַׁת חַיֵּי שָׂרָה

Parashas Chayei Sarah

The Tzaddik's Donkey

עֲשָׂרָה גְמַלִּים מִגְּמַלֵּי אֲדֹנָיו

Ten camels from my master's camels (24:10)

*They could be distinguished from other camels for they
were muzzled when they went out, against theft, lest they
graze in the fields of others*

(Rashi)

R'Chanina ben Dosa owned a donkey which carried him on its back from place to place. One day a band of thieves happened to pass by the *tzaddik's* house and noticed the fine beast. When no one was looking, they seized the rope around its neck and dragged the donkey to their lair, a cave in the mountains.

They brought the animal some barley and water but the donkey bowed its head and refused to eat the food placed before it. It stood in the cave for three days and three nights, refusing to taste one grain of barley. It sensed that the food belonging to thieves had been stolen or at best, had not been tithed (the required *maaser* had not been set aside).

At the end of the three days, one of the thieves said to his friend, "What are we going to do with this donkey who refuses to eat or drink? It must be ill. It won't be long before it dies. Let's set him loose."

The thieves removed the rope around the donkey's neck, led him out of the cave, and left it to make its way as best it could. The donkey began walking. It walked and walked until it reached its master's gate. And there it stood, braying pitifully.

R' Chanina heard the familiar sound and said, "I think that that is our donkey which was stolen from us three days ago. Go and open the gate for it. It must be hungry. Give it some oats and water for it sounds very weak!"

Someone ran out and opened the gate. The poor animal rushed in and went to its place in the barn. But when food was brought and the water troughs were filled, it refused to eat. R' Chanina's son went inside to report this strange behavior to his father.

"Did you forget to set aside *maaser* from the feed? That must be the reason why he will not touch the oats."

Indeed, in the confusion the family had forgotten about *maaser*. When it was duly set aside the starved animal began to eat — and with what an appetite!

(According to *Midrash Rabba Bereishis* 10)

Give Away a Mitzvah?!

גַּם תֶּבֶן גַּם מִסְפּוֹא רַב עִמָּנוּ גַּם מָקוֹם לָלוּן

Both straw and fodder aplenty do we have, and also lodgings
(24:25)

Guests had arrived unexpectedly at the home of R' Levi Yitzchak of Berditchov's father-in-law. R' Levi Yitzchak bustled about, running to the barn and back in order to fetch large piles of straw for the guests to sleep on. He had to go back and forth several times. It was tiring work; the sweat poured down his back. But he did it happily.

"Why must you work so hard?" his father-in-law said. "I can send for a gentile to bring a load of hay in his wagon. It will only cost a few pennies!"

"What?!" said R' Levi Yitzchak. "Am I to give away my *mitzvah* to a gentile — and even pay him for it as well?!"

A Mitzvah for Four Zuzim

גַּם תֶּבֶן גַּם מִסְפּוֹא רַב עִמָּנוּ גַּם מָקוֹם לָלוּן

Both straw and fodder aplenty do we have, and also lodgings
(24:25)

R' Yeshaya of Zochowitz was well known for his *hachnasas orchim*. His hospitality was legendary. When he had guests, he wanted them to really enjoy themselves and eat as heartily as if they were at home.

A group of guests arrived one Friday afternoon, shortly before *Shabbos*. R' Yeshaya went out to welcome them to his home. He showed them to a clean room with fresh towels and clean, comfortable beds. He told them to unpack their things and make themselves at home.

A few minutes before *Shabbos* R' Yeshaya came in and told them, "I know that you were told that you could spend the *Shabbos* here. I charge four *zuzim* a person for a *Shabbos*. This may seem high but for this price you can eat your fill, drink the best of wines and really feel at home."

The men were somewhat surprised but it was too late to change their plans. Oh well, they thought. If they were paying, they might as well take advantage of it and enjoy themselves.

They had a very pleasant *Shabbos* indeed. The food was plentiful and excellent, the wine superb and the host was warm and accommodating. He did everything to make their stay comfortable. They had no regrets, even if they knew that they would have to pay. After *Shabbos* they were given a sumptuous *melaveh malkah* meal which they also ate heartily.

Sunday morning arrived. It was time to leave. When they had gathered all their belongings, the guests went to R' Yeshaya to pay him the four *zuzim*. But to their great surprise, he refused to accept a penny!

"Do you think that I would accept money for doing such a great *mitzvah*?! That I would sell such a privilege for payment?!"

"B-b-but you said on Friday..."

"Never mind what I said on Friday," R' Yeshaya interrupted them. "I only said that I was charging you so that you would feel at home, that you would not feel embarrassed to eat heartily, or to ask for anything you desired. But now — I wouldn't dream of taking money!"

The Rabbi's Condition

גַּם מָקוֹם לָלוּן

Both straw and fodder aplenty do we have, and also lodgings
(24:25)

I t had been a stormy day, a terrible day for traveling. But Reb Baruch had had no choice. The roads had been muddy and the coach had made poor time, reaching Gestinin very late at night. The streets were already dark. It had been a day for huddling around a fire and going to sleep early. There was not a single light in the entire city. What could Reb Baruch do?

He wandered around searching hopefully for a sign of life. He did not want to wake anyone up. Suddenly he spied a single candle lighting up a window. He hurried towards it and reaching the house, knocked hesitantly at the door. It was opened at once by a kindly looking Jew who ushered him in, set him in front of a blazing fire and brought him some warm food and tea. The traveler was grateful.

The solicitous host was R' Yechiel Meir, the rabbi of Gestinin, a scholar who spent his nights as well as his days in Torah study. Since no one had been up, he himself had warmed up food and made a bed for his unexpected guest.

The next morning, the rabbi hushed all the members of his family so that the weary traveler staying with them could sleep his fill. He waited for him to wake up by himself, then took him to the synagogue. Here the stranger learned that he had been lodging by the distinguished rabbi of Gestinin. He felt very embarrassed at having caused this noble person such inconvenience and apologized profusely.

"No, I will not forgive you!" said the rabbi.

The traveler did not know what to do. He again asked his host to forgive him for having caused such trouble. Finally the rabbi agreed. "But only under one condition..."

"And what is your condition?" the visitor asked, full of curiosity.

"The condition is that each time you pass through Gestinin, come and stay with me."

A Member of the Family

גַּם מָקוֹם לָלוּן

Both straw and fodder aplenty do we have, and also lodgings
(24:25)

R' Baruch Mordechai of Warsaw had an open house to anyone who wished to enter. People came and went as they pleased, never asking permission, taking everything for granted. They really felt at home there. And R' Baruch Mordechai certainly did not care. That is how he wanted it!

R' Shabsai Yogel of Slonim described it well: "When R' Baruch Mordechai takes a nap on a couch at home," he said, "it is not as if it were his couch. Rather, it is because he happened to find it unoccupied first, before anyone else lay on it."

R' Baruch Mordechai himself came and went just like the others. He had no special place at the head of the table. He was served his meals just like the rest. He did not want anyone to make a fuss over him.

Small wonder, that when a poor man came to this house and stayed for several weeks, he did not even recognize R' Baruch Mordechai as the master of the house. He thought he was just another guest. Once this poor man turned to R' Baruch Mordechai and asked innocently, "I see that you are a steady guest here. You probably know what is customary here better than I do. Tell me, do you think that they would mind if I stayed a few weeks longer?"

R' Baruch Mordechai shrugged his shoulders and reassured him, "No. I am sure you are welcome here. I have been living here — eating and sleeping — for a long time and no one has ever said anything..."

Easy Work?

מֶה׳ יָצָא הַדָּבָר
It is from Hashem (24:50)

A rich Roman matron once asked R' Yosi ben Chalafta: "In how many days did *Hashem* create the world?"

"Six," came the swift reply.

She continued to ask, "And since then, what has He been doing?"

"He is occupied with arranging marriages: this man's son is to marry that man's daughter..."

"That's work?!" she asked in surprise. "Why, I can do that too! I have many servants and maids. I can match them up in no time!"

R' Yosi replied, "Perhaps, you think that matchmaking is easy work, but *Hashem* considers it as difficult as the splitting of the Red Sea!"

The Roman matron approached her task. She took one thousand servants and a thousand maids, lining them up side by side. Then she began pairing them off, two by two, until she had gone down the entire line. It did not take long.

The next morning she was besieged by complaints. The servants and maids came to her, bruised and beaten, shouting and weeping, "I don't want so-and-so for a wife! I cannot get along with my husband!" And so on. One thousand pairs came before the matron, each one dissatisfied for a different reason.

The woman quickly summoned R' Yosi and said, "Rabbi, I see how right you were and how fine and true is your Torah. Everything that you said is perfectly correct. Matchmaking is not easy!"

(According to *Midrash Rabba, Bereishis* 68:4)

Appeasement

מֶה׳ יָצָא הַדָּבָר

It is from Hashem (24:50)

R' Shmuel Shtrashun was deeply revered by all of Jewry for his brilliance in Torah. But he was also greatly respected for his devotion to the Jewish community. Among his many public activities, he managed a *gemilus chesed (gemach)* free-loan fund for the people of Vilna.

R' Shmuel was very careful in keeping the accounts of his fund. He made certain that people repaid their loans as soon as they were due, else there would not be any funds available for other people to borrow. And he would mark everything carefully in his books.

An ordinary Jew once needed a loan of one hundred rubles for four months. He came to R' Shmuel, received the money and promised to return it on the appointed day.

Four months later, when the loan was due, he went to R' Shmuel's home but did not find the rabbi in. "He is in the *beis medrash*," he was told. The man went there and found R' Shmuel deeply engrossed in a complex subject in the *gemarah*. The man laid the money in front of him. R' Shmuel looked up, nodded, and went back to his study. The man was certain that the rabbi had acknowledged his receipt of the money and went his way.

But R' Shmuel had only nodded automatically. His mind had been on other things. He pored over the *gemarah* for a long time, turning pages back and forth. When he was finally satisfied with the solution, he shut the *gemarah* and put it back on the shelf in the *beis medrash*, oblivious of the money pressed between its pages.

Every week R' Shmuel would go over the *gemach* account books to see which loans were paid up and which still had to be collected. When he came to the name of that Jew he noticed that the loan was still outstanding. He summoned him and demanded that he repay the one hundred rubles.

"But I already paid you!"

"You did not. It is written, here, that you still owe the money."

"I put the money on the table right in front of you! I paid back my debt!" the man insisted. R' Shmuel did not remember. He demanded payment, but the man refused, claiming that he had already paid. R' Shmuel insisted that he appear before a *din Torah*.

All of Vilna learned about this *din Torah*. The man was in public disgrace. How did he dare stand up against the famous scholar? He was, in effect, calling him a liar!

The hearing took place in the *beis din*. Both sides were heard and the scholar's story held more weight. The judges postponed their decision for a later date, hoping that the man would admit that he had not paid back his debt.

The poor man had no sympathizers in all of Vilna. He was considered a stubborn fool, a thief. His good name was undermined; people stopped talking to him; his son could not bear the disgrace and left Vilna altogether. Finally the man was even dismissed from his job. Still, he continued to insist that he had paid back his debt.

Time passed and R' Shmuel happened to need the same *gemarah*. He opened it up and discovered the money, one hundred rubles. For a moment he was puzzled, wondering how such a large sum could have been misplaced there. Suddenly, it all came back to him. This was the missing money which the defendant had insisted he had repaid.

R' Shmuel felt terrible. He had wronged a Jew! He had accused him falsely! Shaken to his core, he quickly summoned the man and said, "How can I possibly make amends for the anguish I caused you? I am prepared to make a public confession to clear your name. But will this be enough? Can this possibly compensate for your suffering?!"

The man stood before the rabbi. His face was gaunt, lined with the ravages of his suffering. He said sadly, "What is done is done. My good name is already ruined. Even if you were to free me of blame, people would not forget that I had once been accused of such a terrible thing. They might think that you had pity on me and wished to clear my name, but they would still consider me a thief and a liar. No, not even a public retraction would help me now. Besides, it would not bring my son back. He left Vilna out of shame."

R' Shmuel was thoughtful for a long time, "How could he help the broken man before him, the man whose reputation he himself had ruined?" Suddenly, he had an idea. "Send for your son. Tell him to return to Vilna. I will take him as a husband for my daughter. This will certainly restore your good name!"

The man was overwhelmed. He had never dreamed of such a wonderful thing. That his son should marry the rabbi's daughter!

The son was summoned back and the engagement took place several days later. The cream of Vilna society took part in the affair. People could not stop talking about the amazing turn of events; they could not help but marvel at the ways of Providence. "It had been decreed from birth that this ordinary man's son was to marry the rabbi's daughter. And how had this been accomplished? Through the mistake about the loan. How amazing were the ways of heaven!"

Black Bread and Potatoes

וַיֵּצֵא יִצְחָק לָשׂוּחַ בַּשָּׂדֶה לִפְנוֹת עָרֶב

And Yitzchak went out for a walk in the field towards evening (24:63)

'Lasuach' — a term for prayer (from 'siach' — speech)

(Rashi)

A Jew burst into the *beis medrash* of Ropshitz in a frenzied hurry. It was already early afternoon and he had not yet *davened shacharis*! He hurriedly put on his *tallis*, took out his *tefillin* and wound the straps around his arm with lightning speed. He swayed back and forth, his lips moving rapidly as he skimmed through the prayers. The entire service was over in less than half a hour. He was hastily winding his *tefillin* and putting them back in the velvet bag when someone came over to him. It was the Rebbe, R' Naftali of Ropshitz.

"Do you have a moment?" he asked. The man nodded, his curiosity aroused. R' Naftali began:

"There was once a poor man who could not afford more than simple black bread and potatoes. He ate this fare, day in and day out and always found his meal ready for him when he returned home from prayers. One time when he came home he found the table bare. 'Oh, you are back already?' his wife said. 'Wait a bit until I prepare your meal.' The man sat down to wait. One hour passed, then another. 'What was taking so long,' he wondered. 'Cooking up a few potatoes was such a simple matter. Perhaps his wife had something special for today, some fish or even some chicken.' He waited eagerly, his mouth watering with expectation. More time passed, but still no food. Finally he became impatient and called out, 'Where is my meal?' His wife hurried out of the kitchen, set the table and brought the same black bread and plate of steamed potatoes that she always served. Her husband was furious. 'For this I had to wait all day?! Could you not have prepared this simple meal early in the morning as you always do?'"

R' Naftali looked at the man before him. "Surely you can apply the moral yourself. If there are some Torah scholars who are accustomed to praying late, it is because they spend much time preparing for these prayers. They purify themselves in the *mikvah*, and collect their thoughts so that they will be able to pray with concentrated fervor. The prayers of these chasidim or scholars are special. They are worth waiting for, so to speak. But you come bursting into *shul* after everyone has long gone with your short, short prayer which is a hasty affair, an inferior thing. Why could you not have said these same casual prayers early in the morning?!"

Seeing Only the Good

וְלֹא עֲצָבוֹ אָבִיו מִיָּמָיו לֵאמֹר מַדּוּעַ כָּכָה עָשִׂיתָ

His father never rebuked him, saying: Why did you do that?
(Haftorah Parashas Chaye Sarah, Melachim I, 1)

R' Zusha of Anipoli was a man who loved his fellow Jew and sought to improve his character through love rather than by scolding him. But R' Zusha had not always been like this.

When R' Zusha was a young man, he was once staying with his teacher, the famous Maggid of Mezeritch. He was alone with the Rebbe when someone came to ask the Rebbe to pray for him.

"I am not doing well at business, Rebbe. I have many expenses and my income does not cover the cost of living. I cannot make ends meet. Please, Rebbe, can't you pray for my success in business?"

R' Zusha looked at the man and his keen eye saw right through him. This man was wealthy enough! He lived very well, had a large house, servants, his own coach. Yet he did not give enough to charity. Nor was he honest in business. He cheated, and did not pay his workers what they were worth. In short, he was not a decent man at all. R' Zusha became angry and said,

"How dare you even stand before the Maggid, who is so holy, when you are so full of sin?! How dare you ask for your selfish desires when you yourself never think of anyone else! You should be ashamed to stand here without having thoughts of repentance for your evil, selfish deeds."

After the man had gone, R' Zusha realized how shamefully he had behaved. He had embarrassed a Jew! He had spoken sharply to a person who had never done him any harm. He shuddered. What a terrible person he was. Why had he not been able to hold his tongue! Who knows if he might not speak out like this again and embarrass other Jews?

The Maggid saw R' Zusha's distress and tried to comfort him. But R' Zusha would not be comforted. "What if this happens again and I am unable to restrain myself?" he wept. The Maggid said,

"Don't worry, dear Zusha. I hereby bless you. May you never again see the evil in a person's soul. From now on you will only see the good in each Jew! You will only be able to love your fellow Jew!"

פָּרָשַׁת תּוֹלְדֹת

Parashas Toldos

The Precious Object

וַיֶּעְתַּר לוֹ ה' וַתַּהַר רִבְקָה

And Hashem harkened unto him and Rivka conceived (25:21)

There was once a woman who was still childless after ten years of marriage. Her husband went to R' Shimon bar Yochai to ask if he might divorce her and marry someone else who could bear children.

R' Shimon said, "Just as you were married in joy and happiness, with a feast, so should you be separated with a feast."

The man arranged a large banquet. He sat with his wife, eating and drinking to his heart's content. In the course of the meal he became a little drunk and said to his wife, "My good woman, you may take anything from this house to keep when you leave me to return to your father's home. Choose any object that is most precious to you."

The woman was clever. As soon as her husband was fast asleep, she ordered the servants to carry him to her father's house.

When he awoke, it was the middle of the night. He looked about at the strange surroundings and asked,

"Where am I?"

At his side, his wife replied, "You are in my father's house. Last night you promised that I could take anything for my own. I could find nothing to take more precious than you, my dear husband!"

The two went back to R' Shimon the following morning. The *tzaddik* stood and prayed that they be blessed with child. And *Hashem*, Who values the prayers of His *tzaddikim*, harkened to his plea and blessed the couple with a child.

(From *Midrash Rabba, Shir HaShirim* 1:31)

Sewing for Heaven's Sake

וַיִּגְדְּלוּ הַנְּעָרִים

And the lads grew up (25:27)

When they turned thirteen — the one turned to the 'batei midrash' and the other turned to idolatry

(Rashi)

"Something must be done about Elazar," people used to whisper to one another in deep concern. "He is so wild, so mischievous. It is not fitting for the son of such a great man as R' Elimelech to behave so naughtily." The people of Lizensk worried, for the Rebbe's son showed no signs of the greatness which his father possessed. What would become of him! Perhaps, they thought, the Rebbe did not realize how willful the child was? Finally a few people got up the courage to speak to the Rebbe about Elazar.

The Rebbe did not seem unduly concerned about the matter. He reassured them and said, "We will wait until his *bar mitzvah*."

The boy approached the age of thirteen. Preparations were made for his *bar mitzvah* and he was to have a new suit. The Rebbe wished the suit to be sewn in his own house; he wanted to supervise the tailoring.

The tailor came to the Rebbe's home to take Elazar's measurements. Then he spread the material out on a large table. Before he began cutting, R' Elimelech said,

"I want this to be a very special suit. I want it to be made from beginning to end with deep concentration; it must be sewn for the greater glory of *Hashem*. When you cut the fabric I want you to say: 'this is *leshem shamayim*, for heaven's sake."

When he reached the work on the shoulders, the Rebbe stopped the tailor and said: "I want you now to say: 'These shoulders must bear the yoke of *Hashem*.' And when you get to the sleeves, you must concentrate intently and say, 'These hands are to labor only for *Hashem*.' By the trousers, you must say, with all your heart, 'Elazar's feet must run only to do *mitzvos* and serve their Creator.' And so on..."

The tailor worked diligently, following R' Elimelech's precise instructions.

When the time came for Elazar to wear his suit for the first time, on the day of his *bar mitzvah* everyone noticed a wonderful transformation. The child who minutes ago had still been playing pranks on his friends suddenly turned serious. A look of holiness rested upon his features. He stood tall and straight, not fidgety like the restless child he had just been. An air of maturity seemed to envelop him as he stood there proudly in his new suit. Now he was a man.

And from that day on Elazar attacked his studies with a new seriousness and devotion until he grew up to become one of the great men of his generation, a leader of Jewry, like his saintly father.

Tears Inside the Tefillin

וַיִּגְדְּלוּ הַנְּעָרִים

And the lads grew up (25:27)

Little Zevi was a child like all the other boys in his class. He learned, played, was sometimes good and sometimes mischievous. No one had any complaints about Zev, for he was an average child. Still, people were somewhat disappointed. They expected the son of the great R' Yechiel Michel of Zlotchov to be something special. Yet he showed no signs of being outstanding in anything.

Little Zev grew up. His *bar mitzvah* approached. The Rebbe ordered his son's *tefillin* from an expert *sofer*-scribe, but asked that the *sofer* bring them to him before inserting the parchment inside the *batim*.

When both the parchment and the *batim* were ready, the scribe came to R' Yechiel Michel so that he could inspect the work. The Rebbe took the *tefillin* in his hand

and suddenly was overcome with emotion. He began weeping, his tears filling the hollow black box. He wept and wept, praying fervently for the future of his dear son. And when the tears overflowed from the black box, he emptied them and stopped weeping.

When the *tefillin* were completely dry the *parshiyos* were inserted. Everything was now ready for the *bar mitzvah*.

When Zev put on his *tefillin* for the first time, he felt a wave of holiness sweep over him. He suddenly became a man, filled with the fear and love of G-d. From that moment onwards Zev was transformed. He began to excel in his studies, for he now had a burning desire to learn more and more, to strive and achieve great heights in Torah. And in time, he became one of the *tzaddikim* of his generation.

All for One Ruble

וַיִּמְכֹּר אֶת בְּכֹרָתוֹ לְיַעֲקֹב

And he sold his birthright to Yaakov (25:33)

"Rebbe! You must help me!" Reb Mottel burst into the *beis medrash* of the Tzaddik of Apta. Tears streamed down his cheeks as the poor man told the Rebbe of his worthy daughter who was getting older and could not get married until he had a decent dowry for her.

'How much do you need?" the Rebbe asked kindly.

A desperate chuckle escaped his throat. "Ha! I have one ruble in my pocket. Here it is! I need one thousand!" He took out a worn coin and held it up.

"Hmmm. One ruble. Very well. That is a beginning. Take your one ruble and buy the first item of merchandise that comes your way. May *Hashem* bless you that your money increase to cover your needs," the Rebbe said, nodding his head. The man understood that he must leave.

"One ruble! What can I possibly buy with one ruble?!" Reb Mottel thought to himself. Yet, he had come to the Rebbe after hearing of his greatness, of the great wonders that he had wrought. He had full confidence in the Rebbe's powers. Still it seemed strange that one ruble could turn into one thousand..., but the Rebbe had given his blessing!

The man started on his way home. He had traveled a long way to Apta and now he was tired. After several hours of travel he decided to stop and rest by a roadside inn. He found himself a seat by a table and sat down. His eyes darted all around the room, studying the scene. Perhaps he would find some merchandise here, as the Rebbe had advised. His eyes hit upon a group of diamond dealers huddled in a corner. Their wares were spread on small squares of special rice paper on the table and they were arguing heatedly. Overcome with curiosity, the poor man edged over and stood by the shoulder of one of the men. The merchant looked up and asked, "Interested in buying something?"

Reb Mottel was about to say "No" but caught himself and changed it to a "Yes." He remembered what the Rebbe had said.

"How much money do you have?" asked the diamond dealer.

He blushed but replied, "I have one ruble." Everyone burst into raucous laughter. What a ridiculous idea — to buy diamonds for a ruble! When the laughter died down, the merchant said,

"I have something to offer you for a ruble."

"Really? What?"

With laughter still bubbling inside him, he said, "I will sell you my portion in *Olam Haba* for a ruble."

"It's a deal!" the poor man blurted out. "But let us make the sale legal and above board. We must draw up a proper document of sale."

The sharp businessmen sitting around the table were enjoying themselves. They had never seen anything like this! How amusing! One rushed to fetch a sheet of paper, another a pen. A third, an expert in legal terminology, dictated the terms of the sale. Soon the contract was ready for signing. Both the buyer and the seller wrote their names. Then two witnesses were asked to verify the sale. Finally, Reb Mottel handed over his last ruble and took the document in exchange. The deal had been transacted.

Reb Mottel returned to his table to the whoops of laughter from all the gem merchants. But he did not care.

Just at that moment a woman entered the inn. It was the merchant's wife. Seeing her husband besides himself with laughter, she asked him what had happened. He pointed to Reb Mottel and said,

"See that poor man there? I just squeezed the last ruble out of his pocket by selling him something worthless. What a fool! Ha! Ha! Ha!"

"What did you sell him?" she asked, full of curiosity.

"I sold him my portion in *Olam Haba*."

He burst into a peal of fresh laughter but froze when he saw his wife's expression.

"The only thing of lasting value that you still have, your tiny portion in *Olam Haba* — you sold? Is nothing holy to you? Is there nothing in this world that you value outside of money? Why, you are no better than a gentile! You vile, miserable creature! I don't want you for a husband! I demand a divorce. I refuse to live with a man to whom nothing is holy, not even his tiny portion of immortality."

He saw that she was dead serious. He tried to wave the matter away, "It was only a joke..."

"That was no joke. It was a proper sale with a document, signatures and witnesses. Oh, no! You meant it! And I refuse to live with a man who denies his portion in the World to Come, little as it may be!"

This was already going too far. He had not dreamed that there would be complications. But his wife was serious about demanding a divorce. Finally an idea struck him. He beckoned to a waiter and asked him to tell the Jew in the corner to come over to his table.

Reb Mottel came and stood before him.

"It was a good joke, wasn't it?" the gem merchant said in a friendly, confidential manner. "You agree that it was only clean fun. Come, let's dissolve our agreement now, like adults. I'll give you back your ruble and you return the document. Surely you need the money more than the silly piece of paper!"

Reb Mottel shook his head. He was not smiling. "I made a serious sale. I have no regrets. For my part, it is a completely valid transaction."

"Do you know what?" the gem merchant said in a silky

smooth voice, "I'll give you a few extra rubles if you give me back the paper."

"No. I am sorry. It is mine. The purchase is legally sound."

"Come now, don't be a fool. How much do you want for that worthless paper?"

"One thousand rubles."

"One thousand rubles? Are you out of your mind? For an insignificant piece of paper? You must be mad!"

"You made the offer, not I. I am content to keep the document."

"All right. Be a stubborn fool. I don't need the stupid paper."

"What do you mean?" his wife shouted. "If you do not buy the document back, I insist on getting a divorce. I demand that we go to a rabbi this very minute!"

"But my dear. It is a ridiculous price: one thousand rubles for a worthless document! Surely you don't mean what you are saying!"

"Of course I mean it! I don't care if you have to pay five thousand rubles. I refuse to go on living with a gentile, a man who denies his portion in *Olam Haba*! That is final!"

The merchant now turned to Reb Mottel and tried to bargain him down. Reb Mottel was adamant. One thousand rubles, not a penny less.

Finally, the merchant dug into his pocket, took out his wallet and counted out one thousand rubles. He handed it over to Reb Mottel who, in turn, gave him the document. In a fit of anger, the merchant ripped it to pieces.

Reb Mottel turned to the woman and told her exactly what the Rebbe had advised, explaining why he had set a price of one thousand rubles. When she heard the story, she was deeply impressed and decided to travel to Apta at once.

The woman entered the Rebbe's study and said, "I am very happy that my husband's money went to such a worthy cause. But I am curious about one thing: was my husband's portion in *Olam Haba* really worth only one ruble?!"

The Rebbe smiled. "When he first sold it, it was not even worth that much! But after he redeemed it for one thousand rubles, his portion suddenly shot up in value. After that *mitzvah* of providing for a poor bride, his portion can no longer be measured even in gold!"

To Enjoy the Fruits

שְׁכֹן בָּאָרֶץ

Dwell in the land (26:2)

Dwell in the land — dig roots in the land. Plant and sow.

(Midrash Rabba)

The Roman emperor Hadrian once set out upon a war in a distant land. On his way there, he and his soldiers traveled through *Eretz Yisrael* and came to a small village near Tiberias. There they noticed an old man working in his garden. The man was toiling with his spade, digging holes and planting young fig seedlings.

The emperor stopped to watch him. The man toiled tirelessly, ignoring the perspiration that rolled down his face and back. He looked at the man's hands: how work-worn they were, full of callouses and, still, the old man worked away.

"Grandfather!" the emperor said. "Don't you think that you have toiled enough in your lifetime? Tell me, how old are you?"

The old man straightened up and replied proudly, "I am one hundred years old, praise *Hashem*!"

"One hundred years old and still planting trees?!" the emperor marveled. "Why do you work so hard? Do you really expect to reap the fruits of your own labor? Do you think that you will live to eat the figs from these little seedlings? Surely you will die before then and others will enjoy the fruits!"

"That doesn't matter," replied the old man with a content smile. "If it be *Hashem*'s will that I die, then I will be happy if others enjoy the fruits. My sons and grandsons will benefit, just as I ate the fruits of the trees which my own father and grandfather planted. That is life."

The emperor and his army continued along their way and reached the front. The war was a long and hard one. Finally, after three years, Hadrian scored a final victory and was able to return home. Again he passed through *Eretz Yisrael* and again he found himself by the orchard near Tiberias. The same old man was in his garden, tending his trees.

But the small seedlings of three years before were now proud, fruit-bearing trees! Large green leaves shed their protection over the juicy green and purple figs.

The old man saw the emperor and his soldiers

approaching. He quickly took a basket and filled it with the biggest, juiciest fruit he could pluck. Then he rushed out to the road and up to the emperor, presenting him with the fruits of his labor. "Your Majesty," he said, "if you recall, I am the same old man whom you met three years ago on your way to war. I was then planting fig seedlings. And today you see me here, still alive, able to enjoy the fruits of my efforts. Here, Your Majesty. Eat and be refreshed."

The emperor was deeply impressed. "I see clearly that your G-d loves you indeed. If He respects you, I will do so too." He turned to his servants and told them to take out the figs and fill up the basket with gold coins.

The servants did as they were bid. In return for his gift of figs, the old man received a basket full of gold!

(According to *Midrash Tanchuma Kedoshim 8*)

Why He Hates

וְאֶת עֵשָׂו שָׂנֵאתִי
And Esav do I hate
(Haftorah Parashas Toldos, Malachi 1)

Turnus Rufus, the Roman, once came to R' Akiva with a question: "Why does *Hashem* hate us, we the descendants of Esav, as the prophet says, 'And Esav do I hate'?"

R' Akiva replied, "Give me until tomorrow to reply."

The next day Turnus Rufus came to R' Akiva for his answer. He asked the sage what he had dreamed the night before.

"I dreamt that I saw two dogs, one of them named Rufus and the other Rufina," the sage replied.

Turnus Rufus was furious. "You dared name two dogs after me and my wife?! I will have your head removed!"

R' Akiva answered. "What is the difference between you and a dog, really? You both eat and drink. You both have children. You both are born and die. Why are you angry that I compared you to a dog? What is the difference, after all?

On the other hand, *Hashem* created the heaven and earth. He stretches out the firmament, supports the upper and lower waters, gives life and takes away life. And yet you take a log of wood and call it god! What arrogance! Do you not think that you deserve to be hated?!"

Turnus Rufus was silent.

A Double Donation

וְעַוְלָה לֹא נִמְצָא בִשְׂפָתָיו בְּשָׁלוֹם וּבְמִישׁוֹר הָלַךְ

And evil was not found upon his lips, in peace and
straightforwardness did he go
(Haftorah Parashas Toldos Malachi 2)

Everyone knew of R' Moshe Bassan's deep love for *Eretz Yisrael.* Everyone knew that since he could not settle there himself, he did his utmost to help the settlement of Jews in the Holy Land by sending them large sums. He had a *pushke* which stood on his table at all times, alongside the many books from which he was always studying. And the people of his congregation, who revered and loved their rabbi, always gave generously to his favorite charity, the poor of *Eretz Yisrael*.

One day a distinguished member of the community entered R' Moshe's study with good news. "I have a *'mazal tov'* coming to me! My wife just had a boy!"

"*Mazal tov*! How happy I am to hear that!"

"I have also come to ask the rabbi to be the *sandak* at the baby's *bris*. It would do me the greatest honor!"

"I would be more than happy to do so but I am afraid that I have a previous engagement on that very day and hour. I have already given my word and will not be able to come. Please forgive me!"

The father looked downcast. But suddenly he had an idea. "I promise to give two hundred *dinar* to the *Eretz Yisrael* fund if you agree to come," he said, certain that R' Moshe would change his mind.

"I have already promised. I cannot break my word," said R' Moshe sadly. He was thoughtful for a few moments. Suddenly he took out his purse and withdrew two hundred *dinar*. He put these into his metal *pushke*, to the man's amazement.

"My dear rabbi, I understand that you are unable to attend. But why did you have to give such a large sum from your own pocket? I was the one who made the offer."

"That is right. But why should the poor people of *Eretz Yisrael* suffer because I could not fulfill your request? Why must they lose two hundred *dinar* for my sake? Since it is my fault, I feel it necessary to contribute that amount."

The man then took out his purse and withdrew two hundred *dinar*, putting them into the *tzedakah* box on the table. "Here, allow me to give the donation in any case. But now, Rebbe, you can take back your money."

"Oh, no! I would not dream of doing that! A gift is a gift! Once it is pledged, it must remain so. But let us hope that in the merit of our double donation the Holy Land will be speedily rebuilt and we can all go there and live! *Amen!*"

For Body and Soul

וְרַבִּים הֵשִׁיב מֵעָוֹן

And he prevented many from sinning
(Haftorah Parashas Toldos, Malachi 2)

The Baal Shem Tov would have liked to remain unknown, to continue a life of solitude, of holy worship. But the time came for him to reveal himself to the world for there was much to be done. Once revealed, the Baal Shem Tov kept close contact with other *nistarim*, *tzaddikim* under the guise of simple laborers or craftsmen who were still hidden to the world but known only to him.

R' Nisan was such a *nistar*. The Rebbe would send him out with missions to save his fellow Jews, in body as well as in soul, and to spread Torah in isolated villages, especially among the simple folk, the unlearned Jews.

Once, when R' Nisan came to the Baal Shem Tov, he was given a difficult mission. He was told that there was a certain Jewish soul which he must save.

"As you know, Count Radziwil owns the village of Harkey where you live. He has a good friend, Pierre Louis, a French nobleman, who is really a Jew who was estranged from his people in infancy. The time has come to return him to his heritage; this is to be your task.

"Each year Count Radziwil invites this Pierre to his estate for hunting." The Baal Shem Tov handed R' Nisan an envelope, saying, "Wait until Pierre arrives. Then open this envelope. It contains your further instructions."

As soon as R' Nisan approached Harkey he noticed great activity. Everyone was getting ready to welcome the count who was returning from their first hunt.

The hunting party returned amid much shouting and noise and turned at once to their lodgings at the home of the local priest. But as soon as the count set foot on the first step, he slipped on the icy stone and fell. In falling the loaded revolver at his side went off, shooting him in the stomach. The count's private physician rushed to his side and tried to stem the heavy flow of blood. He took the count inside, laid him upon a bed and examined the wound but realized that it was too complicated for him to handle. A specialist was summoned at once.

Meanwhile the count lay unconscious, constantly losing blood. He hovered between life and death.

When the Jews of Harkey learned about the terrible accident, they were deeply grieved, for the count was an excellent landlord, a benevolent person who had always treated them fairly. They gathered in their synagogues to pray for his recovery, R' Nisan among them. In the confusion, he almost forgot about the Baal Shem Tov but remembered just in time. He opened the letter with his instructions and read it.

How amazing! The letter described a cure for exactly the type of pistol wound which the count had suffered! R' Nisan returned home, prepared the medicines according to the instructions and then hurried to the home of the priest where the count lay dying.

It was the day after the accident. The count lay unconscious, surrounded by several doctors, all of whom had despaired of his life. R' Nisan entered the house, announcing that he had brought a special cure for the count. He was met by Pierre, the count's French friend. The latter took one look at R' Nisan, at his beard and *payos*, and laughed.

"Do you really think that you can save the count's life when all the specialists have failed to help him?"

"There is no harm in trying, is there?" said R' Nisan. "I have a preparation which I believe will do him much good."

Desperate for anything that might improve his condition, the doctors allowed R' Nisan to approach the sickbed. All stood by while the Jew ministered to the dying count.

First he smeared a special cream on the wound. Then he put several drops of some potent medicine into the count's half-open mouth.

Within minutes there was a marked improvement. The wound stopped bleeding and color returned to the white face. An hour later the count opened his eyes and looked around him.

The doctors rubbed their eyes in astonishment. How

could this be?! It was no less than a miracle! Pierre was the most amazed.

"What miracle drugs did you use to cure the count?" they pressed R' Nisan. He told them all about the Baal Shem Tov and his amazing letter. He told them how this great and holy man was able to cure bodies as well as souls, how he helped people in many miraculous ways.

The doctors listened enrapt. But even more entranced was Pierre Louis, the count's friend. Noting his deep interest, R' Nisan asked to speak to him privately.

The two men entered an adjoining room. R' Nisan told Pierre, "Your name is really Pesach Tzvi. You are named after your mother's grandfather and you are a Jew. As a very young child you were kidnapped and forced to take on the Christian religion. The Baal Shem Tov, in his divine intuition, knew all about you and has sent me to tell you that the time has come for you to rejoin your people. All of your past sins can be forgiven. Repentance is always possible. The decision is yours, however."

R' Nisan had performed his mission. He left Pierre Louis sitting there, thoroughly shaken, deep in thought.

The count's condition improved day by day. It was not long before he was up and about. Soon the hunting party left the village too. Pierre Louis left with it.

A few days later he was back in Harkey. He headed for R' Nisan's humble home and confided to the *nistar* that since the latter's talk with him, he had found no rest for his soul.

"I find that I can no longer eat pork and other foods forbidden to Jews. The hunt no longer appeals to me. My heart yearns to join my brethren. I am drawn to them. Everything that once pleased me seems empty and worthless. I confessed all this to the count and his reaction was most interesting. He said that while he would regret losing me as his friend, he advised me to follow my heart. I should do what my conscience dictated, for that was the only way I would find happiness and fulfillment in life. And so, here I am. I have come to learn about Judaism. I wish to return to my people and become a devout Jew."

Pierre Louis disappeared. He became Pesach Tzvi, the Jew. He remained in Harkey and began studying under R' Nisan. Slowly he began to practice all of the *mitzvos*. Within a short time he had absorbed much Torah and eventually he became a noted scholar.

Who is Fit to Be a Rabbi

וְתוֹרָה יְבַקְשׁוּ מִפִּיהוּ כִּי מַלְאַךְ ה' צְ-בָאוֹת הוּא

"They shall seek Torah from his mouth for He is like an angel of Hashem..."

(Haftorah Parashas Toldos, Malachi 2)

A young man once entered the Chassam Sofer's study. He had a request: "I would like a rabbinical ordination (*smichah*)."

The Chassam Sofer noticed that the man had not kissed the *mezuzah* upon entering the room. It both surprised and disturbed him but he dismissed it as a chance happening. He turned to the young man and said,

"I have no time today. Please come back tomorrow."

The young man left the room. This time, the Chassam Sofer watched him carefully. He again did not kiss the *mezuzah*.

The next day, when he returned, the young man again omitted kissing the *mezuzah* upon entering the room.

The Chassam Sofer then said to him: "I saw you pass through my doorway three times. Not once did you put your hand up to kiss the *mezuzah*. You are not fit to be a rabbi!"

פָּרָשַׁת וַיֵּצֵא

Parashas Vayeitzei

The Dedicated Student

וַיִּשְׁכַּב בַּמָּקוֹם הַהוּא

And he lay down in that place (28:11)

*But during the fourteen years that he studied in the House
of Ever he did not sleep at night, but studied Torah*

(Rashi)

Before Hillel became *Nasi* of his people he was very
poor. Whatever money he earned, he always divided
into two parts. He used half to buy bread for his wife
and children and half to pay the watchmen of the *beis
midrash* to allow him to enter and study Torah from the
great teachers, Shemaya and Avtalyon.

Once, Hillel could find no work and did not earn any
money. It was a Friday. Hillel was distressed that he
could not buy candles, wine and flour for *challos* in honor
of the *Shabbos*. But even more than that, he was unhappy
that he could not enter the *beis midrash* that day and
study Torah from the Sages of the generation.

Hillel passed by the *beis midrash* and thought with
longing, "There, inside, sit my teachers, with their
students at their feet, all studying Torah while I must
remain out here, deprived of that precious Torah. If only
I could just hear what they were saying!"

His longing gave birth to an idea. Quickly he climbed up to the roof and lay down on the skylight. Now, he was able to hear the sweet sounds of Torah study rising from the mouths of Shemaya and Avtalyon. He could even see their faces as they sat in the room, next to the stove.

He lay thus all day, listening avidly. It was the month of *Teves* — the middle of the winter. Yet, he was so enrapt in the beloved Torah which he was hearing that he did not even feel the fierce cold. Night fell and the cold became more intense. Hillel lost consciousness. Snow began falling, slowly covering him. But he no longer felt anything.

Meanwhile, inside the *beis midrash* the rabbis had ushered in the *Shabbos* with joy. They made *kiddush*, ate their *Shabbos* meal and then continued to study until morning.

When dawn broke Shemaya said to Avtalyon, "Avtalyon, my brother, why is it so dark in here today? It is already morning but the light is so dim. Is it so stormy outside that there is no sunlight?"

The two looked up and saw a face staring at them through the skylight.

The *talmidim* rushed up to the roof. They dug through the snow until they found the man who was lying there. They looked at his face and recognized their friend Hillel!

Quickly they took him down and brought him into the *beis midrash*. It was *Shabbos*, yet they washed him, rubbed his body, anointed it with oil and put him near the fire. Hillel began breathing again.

Shemaya and Avtalyan then said: "It is permitted to desecrate the *Shabbos* in order to save a human life. And for Hillel here, who was dangerously sick, it was certainly permitted to desecrate the *Shabbos!*"

Hillel recovered and studied for many years with his great teachers until he, too, became a great Sage, teacher and *Nasi* of all Israel.

(From Tractate *Yoma* 35)

Study and Sleep

וַיִּשְׁכַּב בַּמָּקוֹם הַהוּא

And he lay down in that place (28:11)

But during the fourteen years that he studied in the House of Ever he did not sleep at night, but studied Torah

(Rashi)

The *tzaddik* of Sanz allowed himself only two and a half hours of sleep. And even this small stretch of time was broken up into fragments. He would study, doze off, wake up with a start, wash his hands, study some more, then doze off again and so on, until he had accumulated his two and a half hours of sleep.

The chasidim marveled at him and used to ask, "How can the Rebbe stay healthy on such little sleep?! And even the little sleep that the Rebbe takes is a broken sleep."

The Rebbe would reply, "Sleep is similar to study. Take a chapter in *Shulchan Aruch*. To properly study it and understand it, with commentary, takes a good six hours. But someone with an excellent grasp, with a 'good head' can do it even in two. Thank G-d, I have been blessed with a good head for sleeping. I can get the required six hours of sleep in only two and a half!"

Upon a different occasion, a man once came to the *tzaddik* of Sanz complaining that he suffered from a weakness of character; he enjoyed sleeping. He found it very difficult to get up in the morning. What did the Rebbe suggest? How was *he* able to get along with so little sleep?

"If you find that you are able to sleep, that is your own business! Good for you! As for me — I do not let myself sleep."

Material and Spiritual Needs

וְנָתַן לִי לֶחֶם לֶאֱכֹל וּבֶגֶד לִלְבּשׁ

And He will give me bread to eat and a garment to wear
(28:20)

W hen the grandson of the Baal HaTanya, the Lubavitcher Rebbe, got married, all the great men of the times came to wish the family well. The grandfather rose and offered his own good wishes in the following words:

"May *Hashem* bless you in both the material and the spiritual sense." What he meant, of course, was that he hoped that *Hashem* would amply provide all of his grandson's material needs so that he might better be able to serve *Hashem* spiritually.

One particular rabbi challenged such a blessing, asking, "How is that you put material needs before spiritual ones? Is that proper?"

The Baal HaTanya answered, "I did not do differently than Yaakov Avinu. When he was fleeing his brother Esav, he prayed that *Hashem* watch over him and give him 'bread to eat and clothing to wear'. Then he said, '...and *Hashem* will be my G-d'. He, too, put his material needs before his spiritual ones."

The guest was not yet satisfied. "How can you compare Yaakov's material needs to yours?"

"And how can you compare his spirituality to ours?" came the reply.

The True Owners

וַיְבָרֶךְ ה' אֹתְךָ לְרַגְלִי

And Hashem blessed you for my sake (30:30)

The poor man stood before the Rebbe, at his wits' end. "Rebbe," he wept, "I can bear it no longer. I cannot see my wife in rags, my children hungry and shoeless, my home a wreck. I cannot bear this life of poverty. Help me, Rebbe?"

It was not in vain that R' Yehoshua Heshel of Apta was called the *Ohev Yisrael*. He bore in his heart a deep love for every Jew. And this pitiful man aroused his sympathy. He said,

"Here, take this letter and deliver it to Reb Shalom, a follower of mine who lives in a distant city. He is a wealthy man. I have asked him to give you two hundred rubles to help you out of your predicament."

The poor man thanked the Rebbe heartily and left. He had a long way to travel and no means. He went in part on foot, in part by begging for rides. It did not seem like such a long trip, however, for he was assured of the huge sum of two hundred rubles at the end of his journey. This sum would be enough to set him back on his feet and make him self-supporting, with the help of *Hashem*.

He finally reached his destination. Reb Shalom welcomed him as he would welcome any traveler and invited him to stay for a few days. The poor man rested up from his journey and ate well. Finally he came to his host with the letter in hand.

"I have special greetings to you from the *Ohev Yisrael*. He has sent me here and asked me to give you this letter."

Reb Shalom was overwhelmed. The Rebbe had sent him a message! What an honor! With trembling hands he tore open the envelope. But as soon as he began reading the letter his expression changed to a frown, then to a dark scowl. For you see, Reb Shalom was by nature a very stingy person. Generous in hospitality, a good man, but not able to part readily with any considerable sum of money. He felt a conflict raging within him. He turned to the guest and said,

"Two hundred rubles is a huge sum! I cannot give so much money all at once. Or to one cause. Even if the Rebbe asks it. I'll tell you what, let me give you fifty rubles. That is also a large amount!"

The poor man shook his head. "I can only do what the Rebbe told me. He said I was to get two hundred rubles. I cannot accept any less. It is either that or nothing. It is not a bargaining matter. Either all — or nothing."

Reb Moshe had a terrible conflict. Of course he wished to please the Rebbe. He deeply revered him. Still, on the other hand, two hundred rubles at one time was a huge sum to part with... He was torn in two. Finally, his stinginess won out. He gave nothing.

The poor man left Reb Shalom's house crestfallen. All of his efforts for naught. His hopes were crushed. He had traveled so far and was returning emptyhanded. What a disappointment!

The trip back seemed so much longer and farther. The poor man dragged his feet all the way to Apta and came before the Rebbe, more discouraged than the first time.

He poured out his aching heart. The tears streamed freely down his cheeks. And the *Ohev Yisrael's* own heart went out to this luckless man. "I will give you a letter to a different chasid. This man is not wealthy. I cannot ask him for more than one hundred rubles. But I know that he will not let you leave his house without that amount. Rest assured that he will do everything to raise that sum for you."

The poor man made his way to this second chasid. He was welcomed warmly. The chasid was overjoyed to receive a letter from the Rebbe and after he read it, begged the poor man to remain in his house until he gathered the money together. He borrowed here and there, even sold some of his personal belongings. After a few days he had the entire sum. With joyful heart, he gave it to the poor man, wishing him well.

Meanwhile Reb Shalom was not faring well. From the time that he had rebuffed the poor man, his fortune had taken a turn for the worse. He incurred great losses and in a short while was transformed from a rich man to a beggar. After selling his house to pay his debts, he was left with nothing. Reb Shalom suffered the indignity of having to beg for a crust of bread. It was more than he could bear. He decided to leave his city and wander where people would not recognize him as the formerly wealthy man. As he trudged wearily along strange roads he could not help remembering the poor man who had visited him, asking for two hundred rubles which he really could have spared then, if he had wanted to... Those had been good times. Why had he not obeyed the Rebbe and given him the money?

Suddenly, it struck him that he was being punished. His situation now was a direct result of his stinginess then. Realizing this, he headed straight for Apta, to the Rebbe. He wished to ask forgiveness.

It was a long, arduous trip. He did not always have a roof over his head or bread in his belly. It was cold and windy and his shoes were worn through and through. How well he now understood the plight of that poor man whom he had refused to help. Finally, he reached Apta.

He went right to the Rebbe's house. He would fall down at the great man's feet and beg his pardon. "The Rebbe will surely forgive me," he thought joyfully, "and will bless me. Then everything would be alright again. I will return home and become a rich man once again..." Thus he daydreamed, but was rudely brought back to harsh reality. The Rebbe had sent orders barring him from the court.

It struck Reb Shalom like a thunderbolt. How deep the pain! How bitter the disappointment! He sat down in the corner of the *beis medrash* and began weeping loudly. The chasidim rushed to his side to see if they could help. They asked him what ailed him and he confessed the entire shameful story. What was he to do now?

Someone suggested, "Why don't you stand under the Rebbe's window. Remain there day and night, weeping loudly. Surely, he will ask who is weeping under his window and when he learns that you are truly regretful, he may agree to see you."

Did he have a choice? It was the only way out! Reb Shalom went outside and sat under the Rebbe's window. He wept and wept, without cease. His cries reached the Rebbe's ears and the Rebbe asked about him. When he was told that it was Reb Shalom, he became thoughtful.

"We must have a *din Torah*, he and I. We must lay out our claims before a judge." The Apta Rebbe set a date for the hearing, choosing the saintly Rebbe of Savran as the judge.

The chasidim were curious to see what would happen. The day finally arrived. The courtroom was packed. R' Yehoshua Heshel spoke first. He said:

"I was fated to descend to earth and be rich. But I had no use for riches and so refused to accept such a fate. I said, while still in heaven, that I preferred that my money be distributed among my future chasidim. The heavenly court agreed.

"Reb Shalom here, the man of former wealth, was one of my beneficiaries. He became rich on the money which was to have been mine. I recently asked him to give two hundred rubles to a certain unfortunate man, but when he refused, I decided to take back all of my money which was in his possession and grant it to a worthier man, one who would obey me if I requested charity for a luckless person."

After the Rebbe's explanation the court was utterly still. Reb Shalom stood before the judge, now he flushed, now he turned pale. How he hated himself for not having realized the simple fact that his money had not been his, rather a deposit given to him for safekeeping. Why had he not used the money for its rightful purpose?! He had been a treasurer, but had misused his privilege. He now thought of his family and of how they must now live in poverty and disgrace for the rest of their days. The dreary prospect brought tears to his eyes and he wept unashamedly.

Suddenly the judge's voice rang out with his decision: "The defendant, Reb Shalom, has no claim on any of the money. It did not belong to him in the first place. But, if the Rebbe sees fit to take pity on him, he is free to arrange for Reb Shalom to have enough to keep him from starving or begging, enough to live on decently."

Reb Shalom begged the Rebbe's forgiveness and the Apta Rebbe granted it. Reb Shalom's position improved. And while he never became as rich as he had been, he and his family lived respectfully ever after.

Who Broke the Agreement?

עֵד הַגַּל הַזֶּה

This mound is a witness (31:52)

When Yoav ben Tzruya, King David's commander-in-chief, went to fight against Aram Naharayim, the people came out and said, "You are descended from Yaakov while we are descended from Lavan. Do we not have an agreement between us not to harm one another as it says, 'Let this mound be a witness'? Why, then, have you come to wage war against us?"

Yoav heard this and saw truth in their argument. He returned and came before the king. "Why," he asked, "did you tell me to wage war against Aram Naharayim, if the peace agreement which Yaakov Avinu made with Lavan is still valid?"

David immediately convened the *Sanhedrin* to deal with the problem. They ruled thus: "It is true that there did exist an agreement between Yaakov and Lavan, but it has been violated. Did not Bilam the wicked say: 'From Aram did Balak, King of Moav, lead me'? And Kushan Rishasayim, King of Aram Naharayim, also enslaved the Jews, as it says, 'And the Jews served Kushan Rishasayim...' They are the ones who first broke the treaty."

King David and his general, Yoav, heard the ruling of the *Sanhedrin* and Yoav went forth again to battle against Aram Naharayim.

(According to *Midrash Tanchuma, Devarim 3*)

"Impose Your Fear"

אֲפְגְּשֵׁם כְּדֹב שַׁכּוּל וְאֶקְרַע סְגוֹר לִבָּם

I shall encounter them like a bereaved bear and I shall rend
open their closed heart

(Haftorah Parashas Vayetze, Hoshea 13)

The town of Anipoli was in a turmoil. The duke had been robbed! An enormous sum in money and valuable jewels had been stolen from his safe! The duke did not really suspect the Jews of having any hand in the theft but knew them to be clever and resourceful. If threatened,they would find the thieves, either by their wits or through their prayers. He, therefore, issued a proclamation that if they did not find his money he would banish every last Jew from the town and its environs.

This was terrible! Jews had been making their livelihoods from the lands belonging to the duke. They had rented his fields, taverns, inns, breweries, and had worked his forests! Where would they go? What would they do?

Something had to be done. The *tzaddik* R' Zusha, who lived in Anipoli, was a rebbe who devoted himself to Torah study and who helped his fellow Jews whenever he could. A delegation was sent to R' Zusha to seek his aid.

R' Zusha heard the story and said, "Summon Reb

Shlomo, the rich wine merchant; I wish to speak to him."
R' Zusha knew that Reb Shlomo was a man whom even
the duke respected.

Soon Reb Shlomo was knocking at the door. "Come
in," said the Rebbe. "You know about the danger
threatening the Jewish community living on the duke's
lands. I want you to go to the duke and tell him that I,
Zusha, guarantee to restore his lost money and jewels.
But not right away. He must wait a year's time."

Reb Shlomo delivered R' Zusha's message. The Duke
agreed to postpone the sentence for one whole year.

The year passed swiftly, if suspensefully. The entire
town wondered what R' Zusha had in mind. How was he
going to catch the thief? No clues about the money's
whereabouts came to light, but R' Zusha did not despair.
On the day before the ultimatum, he sent a message to
the duke asking that he gather all of his house servants
in his courtyard the next day. He, R' Zusha, would come
and fulfill his guarantee.

The appointed hour arrived. The duke gathered his
servants. All, but one, were present. The groom was
missing. He was in the stable, tending to the horses.
They fetched him at once.

R' Zusha now looked piercingly at each one, then at all
of them together. He then began shouting, "*Uvechen ten
pachdecha* — impose Your fear *Hashem*...*"

Immediately, the groom confessed, "I did it! I took the
money and jewels." He ran to the stable, returned with
his loot and laid it before the duke. The duke was
overjoyed. He thanked R' Zusha heartily and, thereafter,
treated the Jews with new respect.

The Miser Pays

אָמְרוּ אֵלָיו כָּל תִּשָּׂא עָוֹן וְקַח טוֹב

Say unto Him: forgive all sin and accept goodness
(Haftorah Parashas Vayetze, Hoshea 14)

R'Meir of Premislan was such a holy man that many other great men came to seek his advice and blessing. A certain *tzaddik* once came to R' Meir, asking for his blessing because he planned to settle in *Eretz Yisrael*. R' Meir listened and then said,

"And how do you expect to raise the money for this journey?"

"I hope to visit some relatives. When I tell them of my plans, I am sure that they will help me raise the money."

R' Meir was sunk in thought. He seemed disturbed. "The idea does not appeal to me at all. You will be wasting months of precious time which could be far better devoted to Torah study. But I see that you are determined to go. Let me suggest something: why don't you stay here with me for some time first? I guarantee to raise the money for your traveling expenses.

The visitor thought it over, then decided to accept the offer. The Rebbe did not dismiss him but told his *shammash* to show in the next person who was waiting to see him.

A rich man opened the door and was about to enter when suddenly he spied the man already there. He hesitated on the threshold. Still, the *shammash* had told him to enter. Was there a mistake? He stood there, not knowing whether to advance or retreat. The passing moments seemed like an eternity. Finally R' Meir spoke, telling him to enter.

"I have a story to tell you," he said, turning to the visiting *tzaddik*, "but I would like you to hear it too," he continued, turning now to the rich man. "It has a worthwhile moral that will do you both good.

"Many years ago there lived a very prosperous Jew who owned much property. But Reb Moshe was a very stingy person, a miser. He never let a person into his home. If a poor man came knocking at the door, begging for something to eat, he would tell him to go to his neighbor, Reb Matisyahu, a worthy, G-d fearing Jew. "He will feel far more comfortable there," Reb Moshe would say to himself.

And, indeed, this was true. While Reb Matisyahu was not a man of means like his wealthy neighbor, still, his family always had food on their table. And there was always room for one person more, no matter how shabby or dirty the visitor. Reb Matisyahu's home and heart were big enough for everyone in need.

All of the townspeople felt a deep respect for Reb Matisyahu. He was so good! So kind! But if you think that they held him in higher esteem than the stingy Reb Moshe, you are wrong! It is human nature to respect a man with money and they all treated Reb Moshe with a special reverence, even though they knew how stingy he was.

The injustice of this caused a turmoil in heaven. The angels came before the heavenly court demanding that Reb Moshe be stripped of his wealth and that these riches be given to none other than Reb Matisyahu, who had never denied anyone his help or hospitality. But before the sentence was carried out, Eliyahu Hanavi came before the court and said, "A person should not be judged just by hearsay. I will descend to earth and give Reb Moshe one last chance. I must see if he really is such a miser."

Eliyahu disguised himself as a poor man and descended to earth. He knocked on Reb Moshe's door. A servant answered. When he saw the poor, ragged, shivering man he shooed him away. "Quick, begone! Go, before my master sees you. He is a mean, cruel person. If he finds you here he will throw both of us out of the house." He tried to slam the door shut but the poor man had his foot in the door. "I won't take anything. Just let me warm up by the stove for a few minutes. Don't you see how cold it is outside?"

They were still arguing, when Reb Moshe himself arrived. "What's going on here?" he asked. "What do you want?" he demanded of the ragged stranger.

The servant was so terrified at having been caught speaking to a beggar that he was struck dumb with fear. But the stranger showed no awe of the master.

"I was asking if I could come in and warm up. I wanted a small glass of *shnaps* for my freezing bones."

"You must be out of your mind! This is not a hotel nor a charity hostel!" He turned to his servant saying, "Throw this man out at once!"

Even if he had wanted to be kind, the servant was forced to take the poor man by the lapels and turn him out the door. He shut it tightly behind him.

Eliyahu Hanavi stood outside in the freezing weather, weeping, pleading to be let in just for a few minutes. When he saw that there was no reaction from within,

that Reb Moshe had hardened his heart and was ignoring him, he really wept. He wept for Reb Moshe's soul.

Eliyahu returned to the heavenly court. He did not have good news. There was nothing he could say in Reb Moshe's defense. The case rested. Reb Moshe would have to lose his fortune, as had been ruled.

R' Meir of Premislan continued his story after a brief pause. He raised his voice for emphasis.

"When I, Meir, heard of this sentence, I rushed forward to defend this Reb Moshe. How can one mete out such dire punishment without warning? I asked the heavenly court. I would warn Reb Moshe, I declared. I would not let him be trapped like a poor helpless fly in a spider web. Every Jew deserved a second chance! I would be the court's messenger. If Reb Moshe agreed to give four hundred rubles to this Jew, here, for his traveling expenses to *Eretz Yisrael,* and if he resolved to mend his ways, he would get his second chance. But if," and here he lowered his voice, "G-d forbid, he ignored this warning and persisted in his stingy, evil ways, he would lose his entire fortune and would become dependent upon the kindness of others for the rest of his days!"

R' Meir was silent. Turning to the rich man still standing in the door, he continued, "Reb Moshe is here right now. Let us ask him what he says."

Reb Moshe could not speak. He burst into tears, then fell to the floor in a faint. The Rebbe and the visitor tried to revive him. When he came back to consciousness, he turned to the Rebbe, saying, "You are so right, Rebbe. I have sinned! I have been evil! But I will turn over a new leaf, I promise. But please have mercy!"

He fumbled in his pocket and drew out his purse. He counted out four hundred rubles and gave it to the other man. "Please," he begged, "when you reach Jerusalem, pray for me!"

With the four hundred rubles the *tzaddik* and his family were able to go directly to *Eretz Yisrael* without delay.

As for Reb Moshe, his home became an open house for all wayfarers, troubled people, beggars. His reputation as a great *baal tzedakah* traveled far and wide and he used his great wealth to help his less fortunate brethren in every way.

פָּרָשַׁת וַיִּשְׁלַח

Parashas Vayishlach

One Eighth of an Eighth!

קָטֹנְתִּי מִכֹּל הַחֲסָדִים

I am unworthy of all the kindnesses (32:11)

My merits have been depleted through the kindnesses which You did for me.

(Rashi)

R' Moshe was an extremely modest and humble person. He was famous for his self-effacement. His chasidim, who gloried in their great leader, wanted him to assert himself more, as befitted a leader.

"Rebbe," they would say. "In Tractate *Sotah* it states that a Torah scholar should have one eighth of an eighth of pride. Where, then, is your pride, Rebbe?"

Replied R' Moshe, "You are mistaken. The Sages meant exactly the opposite of what you think. Pride, under all circumstances, is an evil trait. A Torah scholar should always bear this in mind. He should remember what is written in the eighth verse of the eighth *parshah Vayishlach.* Yaakov Avinu says: 'I am too small for all the favors...' Is this pride, or is it humility?"

The Thighbone's Mission

הַצִּילֵנִי נָא... מִיַּד עֵשָׂו

Please save me... from the hand of Esav (32:12)

Caesaria, or Kaysarin, a Roman city in *Eretz Yisrael* on the Mediterranean coast, had a large Jewish population. The gentiles in Kaysarin persecuted the Jews constantly and were always slandering them before the Roman rulers.

Once R' Yitzchak ben Elazar, one of the great Sages living in Kaysarin, was walking along the seashore when he stumbled over some sharp stones. He turned aside and took a steep path when he heard a rustling noise. A strange object was rolling along the road towards him. When it approached, he saw that it was a round thighbone, rolling down the incline like a ball.

"I had better bury it," he thought, "lest someone walking along this narrow path stumble over it and fall." He bent over and hid the bone in a small crevice between the sharp rocks along the road.

He had not gone more than a few steps when suddenly the thighbone slipped from its place and was again rolling down the path. R' Yitzchak realized that he had not thrust it in securely enough. The wind must have dislodged it from its place.

He looked around for a deeper crevice and wedged the bone in tightly. He continued along his way when that very thighbone, which he had wedged in so tightly just a few minutes ago, began rolling down the path again!

R' Yitzchak now understood that the bone was fulfilling a special mission and so he no longer sought to hide it. Just then, a messenger from Rome came running by bearing a pouch of important letters from the emperor for the governor of Kaysarin.

The messenger was speeding along when suddenly he stumbled over something. He slipped on that very thighbone, fell head over heels down the craggy cliff to the shore below, and died.

Jews who were passing by saw the body. They examined the courier's clothing and belongings in the hope of finding some identifying marks or papers. They found a whole satchel full of documents which he had been carrying for delivery. They read them and learned that they were harsh decrees issued by the Roman emperor against the Jews of Kaysarin!

These documents never did reach the governor. The Romans thought that the pouch had fallen into the sea. And by the time the emperor turned his attention to Kaysarin again, the Jews had succeeded in appeasing him with gifts — and he abolished the decrees.

(According to *Midrash Rabba Bereishis 10:8*)

The Hungry Lions

אִם תִּהְיוּ כָמֹנוּ לְהִמּוֹל לָכֶם כָּל זָכָר... וְהָיִינוּ לְעַם אֶחָד

If you be like us to circumcise every male... And we will be as one nation (34:15,16)

A gentile king once turned to R' Tanchum and suggested, "Let both of our nations unite and form one single nation."

R' Tanchum replied, "Very well! But we Jews are circumcised. Since we cannot be like you, you must circumcise yourselves so that you can be like us!"

The king realized that R' Tanchum had bested him. Annoyed, he said, "You have defeated me with your words. But the law requires that whoever defeats the king be thrown to the lions' den."

He summoned his servants and ordered them to throw the Jew to the lions. And so they did. But wonder of wonders! The lions faced R' Tanchum and looked at him, but would not touch him!

An apostate who was present refused to acknowledge this great miracle. He came to the king and said: "Your Majesty, apparently the lions are not hungry now. That is why they refuse to touch the Jew!"

"Very well," said the king. "Let us make an experiment and see if the lions are hungry or not." He quickly turned to his servants and told them to throw that apostate right into the den.

The wicked apostate was thrown to the lions. Without delay, they pounced upon him and devoured him with the greatest of appetite.

(From Tractate *Sanhedrin 78*)

The Precious Stone!

הָסִירוּ אֶת אֱלֹהֵי הַנֵּכָר אֲשֶׁר בְּתֹכְכֶם

Cast off all foreign gods from your midst (35:2)

R' Yitzchak was not blessed with children. He prayed and yearned for a son, but in vain.

R' Yitzchak was a gem merchant by profession. He

bought and sold precious jewels for the ornaments of rich noblemen and their wives. He owned one particular jewel, a sapphire. It was large and perfect, a truly rare gem.

There were two other stones exactly like this one. But they belonged to the king. They served as the eyes of an idol in the king's palace.

Once one of the stones fell and could not be found. When the king heard that there was only one other such stone, he quickly sent a messenger to R' Yitzchak, telling him to pay whatever price the Jew wanted.

"The king will give you one thousand *ducats!*" said the messenger. When R' Yitzchak learned that the king wanted it for his idol, he refused to sell. "My stone is not for sale, not even for a million *ducats!*" he said. The messenger was undaunted. "The king gave me explicit instructions to return with the gem. If you refuse to sell it, he will take it by force. The king will kill you."

"Well, in that case," said R' Yitzchak hesitantly. "I will sell it to the king. But I wish to bring it to him myself."

R' Yitzchak was stalling for time. He did not know what to do. Was he permitted to sacrifice his life? Did he have to? He sailed together with the king's representative and all through the trip he prayed for divine guidance. He certainly did not want to give his gem for the king's idol! Was there any way out? Suddenly he had an idea.

He began extolling the beauty of his gem to the king's messenger. Its magnificence was blinding, he insisted. It was the most splendid gem ever a human eye beheld! It sparkled like a thousand suns!

The messenger was curious to see the gem. He begged R' Yitzchak to show it to him. At first R' Yitzchak refused, saying that it was so precious, he did not want anything to happen to it.

"But I will be very careful! I assure you!" said the curious man.

Finally, R' Yitzchak, with a show of reluctance, agreed. He took out the case that held the jewel and opened it up carefully. Suddenly there was a brilliant blaze as the sapphire caught the light and reflected it; it was breathtaking. "It is beyond my greatest expectations!" the king's messenger said with the deepest awe. "Let me hold it just for one second. I will cherish this moment for the rest of my life!"

At first R' Yitzchak refused but then agreed to let him hold it for just one instant. As the messenger was about to hand it back, R' Yitzchak's hand shook purposely — and the gem fell into the sea!

R' Yitzchak gave a hysterical cry. "My jewel! My precious gem! My entire fortune is lost! What shall I do!"

He threw himself down on the deck crying, "I have lost all my money in one foolish moment! Oh, why did I agree to take it out and show it! What a fool I am! It were better that I should die! The king promised me one thousand *ducats* and special privileges for me and my children forevermore! Alas! Now I have lost everything!"

All of the passengers crowded around him. When they learned of his tragedy they tried to comfort him but he pretended to be completely broken by his loss. When the ship finally docked, some kind passengers accompanied R' Yitzchak to the king to explain what had happened.

"I would indeed have paid him one thousand *ducats* for the gem. But now he does not deserve a single coin. It was his poor luck." Still, seeing how hard R' Yitzchak took his loss, the king arranged to pay his fare back home.

R' Yitzchak returned home, much poorer but greatly relieved. When he got off the ship he met Eliyahu Hanavi who said to him, "Since you sacrificed your entire fortune so willingly rather than have the stone adorn an idol, *Hashem* has taken mercy on you and will repay you with a precious stone, a son who will enlighten the eyes of all Israel until the end of all generations!"

The following year, at the same time, R' Yitzchak's wife gave birth to a son. They named him Shlomo. He is the famous R' Shlomo Yitzchaki or Rashi. And his commentaries illuminate the eyes of all Jewry to this very day and will continue to do so for all time!

The Neighborhood Builder

חֶסֶד וּמִשְׁפָּט שְׁמֹר וְקַוֵּה אֶל אֱ-לֹהֶיךָ תָּמִיד

Keep guard on kindness and justice, and put your trust in Hashem always
(Haftorah Parashas Vayishlach, Hoshea 12)

The group of young *yeshivah* students walked through the silent city streets. It was already late at night; the streets were dark and deserted. Finally, one of them stopped in front of a large house that stood away from the street, surrounded by a thick lawn and flowerbeds.

"This is the house. Come, let us knock," one of them said.

"But it is very late, almost midnight. There aren't any lights on. We will be waking everyone up!" said another.

"What should we do?" asked a third.

"We must wake them up. That is what Reb Moshe said. Without Reb Berel, his daughter's wedding cannot take place." The speaker pressed the bell. It pealed through the house but there were no answering footsteps. He pressed it again, insistently. No reaction from inside.

"This is very strange! I think we should force our way in. Maybe something has happened to Reb Berel and his family?" someone suggested.

They tried the door. To their amazement, it was open and they walked in. Fearfully, they walked through the silent corridor. Suddenly, the first man cried out,

"Stop! Look, there's bundle here on the ground. Oh! It's a man!"

Someone struck a match. It revealed the body of Reb Berel himself. He lay on the ground and beside him lay his wife. They were bound and unconscious.

The young men quickly untied Reb Berel and his wife and revived them. When he came to, Reb Berel said, "Thank G-d that I am alive! It is a true miracle! But who are you? What are you doing here?"

"We are Reb Moshe's messengers. He sent us here to fetch you to his daughter's wedding. He insisted that you come."

Reb Berel gave a huge sigh of relief. "It was the *mitzvah* of *hachnasas kallah* that saved me!" He stood up and walked around his house. Everything was in shocking disorder. "Thieves broke in and tied us up. They beat us unconscious and would have ransacked the house had you not come in the nick of time! Thank you, my dear young men! You saved me!"

"Do you think that you can still come to the wedding? Reb Moshe insisted that you come. It's very late, after midnight, but I know that he is still waiting for you. If you can, that is..."

"By all means!" replied Reb Berel. "I will certainly come for Reb Moshe's sake. It is thanks to him that I was saved." He followed the group of young men and found Reb Moshe still at the wedding hall, although the other guests had already left.

"I must tell you what happened," said Reb Berel. "It is a true miracle.

"This story really begins a few months ago. It was the day after *Pesach*. I met Reb Moshe walking down the street. He looked very upset. I wished him 'good morning' and asked him if anything was wrong. He sighed weakly, explaining that his daughter was to be married right after *Shavuos* but he did not have a penny to spare.

"'How much do you need?' I asked him. He sighed again. 'Two hundred gold coins.' It was a considerable sum but I told him not to worry. On the spot I took out my purse and gave him three hundred. 'It is my pleasure to help you out. But don't forget to invite me to the wedding! I want to be there and wish you a personal '*mazel tov*'.

"I knew that the wedding had been scheduled and that invitations had been sent. But I received no invitation. I was surprised. But, Reb Moshe, you remembered before it was too late, on the very night of the wedding. You sent this group of young men to fetch me, to keep your promise. And this was the very night that the thieves had planned to break into my house. Who knows what they would have done had they not heard the young men coming. They might have murdered us!

"Do you see, this is exactly what the wisest of all men, King Shlomo, taught: 'Cast your bread upon the waters for in the fullness of days you will find it.' Thanks to the money that I gave Reb Moshe, money that I can spare, thank G-d, my life, my family and my fortune were spared!"

Reb Berel had an announcement to make, "I have long thought about going to settle in *Eretz Yisrael*. Now my mind is made up. I will go to Jerusalem and build homes for the poor, homes for Torah scholars. And I hope that this gesture, this good deed, will bring *Mashiach* all the sooner, speedily and in our day!"

"*Amen!*" everyone shouted in chorus.

Reb Berel kept his word. He settled in Jerusalem, near the large square called *Kikar HaShabbat*. Here he built a complex of houses which bears his name to this very day — *Batei Orenstein*. Its founder— Berel Orenstein whose life was spared and who expressed his thanks to *Hashem* in this fine way.

False Scales

כְּנַעַן בְּיָדוֹ מֹאזְנֵי מִרְמָה... כָּל יְגִיעַי לֹא יִמְצְאוּ לִי

Canaan has false weights in his hand... In all my labor you
will not find a sin in me
(Haftorah Parashas Vayishlach, Ovadyah 1)

R' Moshe of Pshevorsk sometimes traveled to various villages. Once he arrived at a town where the businessmen shared a common fault — they were not careful with weights and measures. He gathered all of the townspeople to his sermon, then said:

"Surely you know what our Sages taught in Tractate *Sotah*: 'A person is measured up by the very same yardstick which he uses.' If he is a businessman and uses false weights, then after death, his good deeds are also weighed on a false scale, and he is shortchanged. He loses out by the very same measure!"

Upon a different occasion R' Moshe arrived in Cracow. Here he learned that the rich men in synagogue had the wicked trait of pledging large sums on *Shabbos* but when the *gabbaim* came to redeem their pledges, they only gave small sums, a few pennies!

That *Shabbos*, at the *shalosh seudos* meal, when all the rich men were gathered in the synagogue, R' Moshe got up to speak:

"Surely you know that whenever a Jew does any act, he creates an angel. When he does a *mitzvah*, he creates a good angel. But when he sins, he also creates an angel, a wicked one. By making pledges to charity and not fulfilling them, one creates angels, false angels. After a person dies, all of his angels are gathered to testify. The false ones testify falsely. They lie! And once they lie, who knows what they can invent! They can incriminate a person far beyond his true sins! And so my friends, beware!"

When Yaakov Wars

מֵחֲמַס אָחִיךָ יַעֲקֹב תְּכַסְּךָ בוּשָׁה

From the theft of your brother Yaakov will you be covered with shame
(Haftorah Parashas Vayishlach, Ovadyah 1)

Times were difficult for the Jews of Poland and Galicia. They were stripped of all civil rights and restricted in countless ways. Wherever they turned, whatever they set their hand to — they were constantly thwarted by the envious, anti-Semitic nobility: the local landlords or *pritzim*, as they were called. These counts and dukes held unlimited power in their private estates. They could throw Jews into jail without fair trial, could pass laws, impose taxes and do anything they desired. They were limited only by their own evil imaginations. And the Jews suffered in silence, hoping and praying for the best.

But not everyone was willing to accept the degradation and continuous exploitment. Some Jews wished to take the law into their own hands; they wanted to fight back.

Once, when the police came to search the Jewish section for smuggled goods, they were met with resistance. A group of young Jewish hotheads would not let them in and there was a skirmish. The Jews drew pistols and fired, wounding and killing several policemen. Soon the entire Jewish quarter was cordoned off by police. A constant watch was imposed and the Jews were threatened that if they did not hand over the murderers, the entire section would suffer. The police would stage a pogrom.

This was the signal for bloodthirsty gentiles to swarm to the Jewish quarter. They had been given a green light: police sanction. They were just awaiting the signal to rob, plunder, destroy, and kill. Strangely enough, it was the local bishop, a close friend and admirer of R' Menachem Mendel of Liska, the rabbi of the city, who restrained the hordes.

The chief of police, accompanied by the bishop, entered the ghetto and went directly to the home of the Lisker Rebbe. The bishop pleaded that he produce the murderers. That was the only way to calm the excited mob. The chief of police was not so gentle. He warned that he would not be able to restrain the mob much longer. His words and his harsh tone put terror in the heart of the Rebbe.

As the three men stood there, a young child, the rabbi's precocious son who would later become the famous R' Naftali of Ropshitz, addressed the bishop, saying with childlike self-confidence,

"Excuse me, Your Excellency the bishop, if I speak my mind forthrightly. If the murderers are Jews, then it is the landlords and the nobility who are to blame. It is stated in the Book of *Ovadyah*, 'Because of the wrath of your brother Yaakov you shall be covered with shame.' The explanation is as follows: it is generally agreed throughout the world that Jews by nature are not murderers; they are not shedders of blood. Jews were the first to accept the Ten Commandments, one of which is 'Thou shalt not kill.' They know that murder is punished by the same taking of life. But the descendants of Esav do not hesitate to kill. They live by the sword, as they were blessed by the patriarch, Yitzchak. Furthermore, Yaakov is well aware that Esav is far mightier than he and submits to his cruel blows, as it says, 'My back did I expose to the striker and my cheek to the bruiser. I did not hide my face from abuse and spitting.'

"Thus, throughout the years of our exile we have accepted suffering and contained the pain within us. But if it did happen that our suffering reached a peak and overflowed its bounds so that some of our people could no longer restrain themselves from striking back — this is only a sign that Esav's wickedness has also exceeded its limits. The Jews were no longer able to withhold their anger in the face of Esav's cruelty. Thus Esav is to blame; he should hide his head in shame. For if Yaakov has become a murderer, then it is Esav who should cover himself in shame. He has reduced Yaakov to such a disgraceful state!"

The boy's words impressed and convinced the bishop. He succeeded in persuading the chief of police to leave the rabbi's house and not bother the Jews.

פָּרָשַׁת וַיֵּשֶׁב

Parashas Vayeishev

The Ear of the Right Person

וַיֹּאמֶר לוֹ הִנֵּנִי

And he said to him: Here I am (37:13)

*He was eager to fulfill his father's bidding even though he
knew that his brothers hated him.*

(Rashi)

The two great Sages, Ilfa and R' Yochanan, sat and
learned in the *beis midrash* for many years. But as
time passed, all of their money was used up and their
families were on the verge of starvation.

Finally, one said to the other, "Let us go out and find
some way to earn a bit of money to keep ourselves alive."

They left the *beis midrash* and left the city. They began
to feel hunger pangs and sat down to eat the remainder
of the food in their sacks, beside a decrepit stone wall of
a ruined building.

Suddenly R' Yochanan heard two angels talking on the
other side of the wall.

"Let us push this wall down and bury the two men
alive," said one. "For they forsake Torah study and
pursue affairs of the moment of making a living."

But the other replied, "Leave them be! Fortune smiles
on one of them."

R' Yochanan heard them and asked his friend, Ilfa, "Did you hear anyone talking just now?"

"No, I didn't hear a thing."

R' Yochanan thought to himself: "Since I was the one who heard the angels speaking, I must be the lucky one." He got up and said to Ilfa, "I am returning to the *beis midrash* to study some more Torah. I will fulfill the verse, 'For the poor shall not perish from the land.' I am prepared to live a life of poverty and distress for the sake of Torah."

Each went his separate way. Ilfa engaged in business while R' Yochanan returned to study Torah. It was not long before the position of *rosh hayeshivah* became vacant and R' Yochanan was chosen to fill this coveted office. Aside from honor and Torah, R' Yochanan also attained great wealth.

This goes to teach you that heavenly announcements are heard by the people who are directly involved. Thus only Reuven heard the heavenly voice. That is why he risked his life to save Yosef from his brothers.

(From Tractate *Taanis 21*)

The Snake That Bit

וַיַּשְׁלִכוּ אֹתוֹ הַבֹּרָה

And they threw him into a pit (37:24)

It contained snakes and scorpions

(Rashi)

A certain village was once beset by a snake which caused untold damage to its inhabitants. The townspeople, in their despair, came to R' Chanina ben

Dosa for help.

He said, "Show me the entrance to the snake's lair."

They took R' Chanina to the snake's lair. R' Chanina placed his heel over the opening. The snake bit the heel and died at once.

R' Chanina took the dead snake, wound it around his shoulders and walked into the *beis midrash*. He turned to his disciples and said, "Look here and take note: it is not the snake that kills but the sin that causes death!"

From then on, it was said, "Woe to a man who meets up with a snake and woe to the snake that meets up with R' Chanina ben Dosa!"

(According to *Tractate Berachos 33a*)

R' Simchah Bunim's Prayer

וַיְבָרֶךְ ה' אֶת בֵּית הַמִּצְרִי בִּגְלַל יוֹסֵף

And Hashem blessed the house of the Egyptian because of Yosef (39:5)

Before R' Simchah Bunim became rabbi of Pshischa, he earned his living as a lumber merchant, working for the famous and wealthy man, Reb Dov Ber Zitkover.

Once R' Simchah Bunim took a large shipment of wood from Warsaw to Danzig where a large trade fair was being held. By the time he reached Danzig, the price of wood had fallen drastically. All of the other lumber merchants were forced to dump their merchandise at a great loss. He decided to hold on to his goods and wait for the price to rise again, even though his financial situation could ill afford the delay.

When his condition became critical, he lifted his voice in prayer, saying, *"Hashem*, we see that Potifar's house was blessed in Yosef's merit. I cannot begin to compare myself to Yosef, but neither can I compare my master, Reb Dov Ber, to Potifar. Let me plead, therefore, that you help my employer and bless him, as you did Yosef!"

His prayers did not go unanswered. As soon as the words were out of his very mouth a lumber merchant rushed in to the room, announcing that, somehow, the price of wood had just soared again. R' Simchah Bunim was able to sell the wood at a great profit for Reb Dov Ber!

Suffering in Prison

וַיְהִי שָׁם בְּבֵית הַסֹּהַר, וַיְהִי ה' אֶת יוֹסֵף

And he was in the prison, and Hashem was with Yosef
(39:20,21)

R' Avraham Yaakov of Sadigura, whose followers numbered in the thousands, had been thrown into jail upon a false charge. As if this were not bad enough, the warden had a particular hatred for Jews and wished to make him suffer as much as possible. He put him together with a rough, crude, violent criminal who, like the warden himself, was a sworn anti-Semite.

The chasidim could not bear to see the suffering of their beloved, revered Rebbe. They did everything they possibly could to win his release through the accepted legal and political channels but meanwhile they still wanted his stay in prison to be as comfortable as possible. They finally gained permission to bring a comfortable, upholstered couch into the cell. His cellmate, the hardened criminal, could not abide this. To make the Rebbe's sleep uncomfortable, he etched the sign of a cross on the couch.

When he saw this, the Rebbe refused to lie on the couch but stood on his feet all the time. His cell mate made the best of the opportunity, lying on it day and night.

As if these troubles were not enough, the Rebbe was also disturbed by a monastery which was situated right next to the prison. All day long the bells rang and the monks could be heard at their prayers. In order not to hear them, the Rebbe put his fingertips into his ears. Thus he stood, uncomfortable but uncomplaining, his lips murmuring prayers to *Hashem*. This irked the criminal no end and he constantly taunted the Jew, disturbing him and making prayer almost impossible. The Rebbe complained to the warden but his pleas fell on deaf ears. Not only did the warden fail to rebuke the prisoner, he actually urged him on! Both gentiles shared a sadistic pleasure in seeing the holy Jew suffer.

The cellmate hardly needed encouragement, but with the warden on his side, he tormented the Rebbe even more openly than before.

Once, when the Rebbe was standing in prayer with his cellmate tormenting him as usual, the latter suddenly gave a cry and sank to the floor, screaming, "Help! Help!"

The prison guards and the warden came rushing to see what was wrong. The criminal begged, "Take me out of this cell. If I remain together with that rabbi a minute longer I will surely die!"

Perplexed by the strange request, the guards looked towards the warden for orders. But he too suddenly fell to the ground and began writhing in pain, just like the prisoner.

He, too, begged to be taken out. He felt that the Jew's presence was causing him the excruciating pain. The two men were carried out of the cell and felt sudden relief. They realized that the Jew was a holy man and that they must not torment him any longer. And from then on the Rebbe received the best of care. Everyone in the prison stood in awe of the holy man and, until the day that he was released, treated him with utter respect.

The Prison's Black Van

וַיִּתֵּן חִנּוֹ בְּעֵינֵי שַׂר בֵּית הַסֹּהַר

And Hashem gave him favor in the eyes of the prison warden
(39:21)

It is the custom in Russia that political prisoners are transported to and from jail in a special 'black van' to denote that they betrayed their motherland. One time R'

Shneur Zalman of Liady, the *Baal HaTanya*, was denounced by his enemies and accused of treason. He was sentenced to serve time in a special jail in a distant city and had to be transported there by this infamous black van.

The Rebbe behaved like a good prisoner throughout the journey. But on Friday afternoon he made a special request; could he and his guards not rest over *Shabbos* and continue afterwards?

His simple plea was rejected. The wagon continued traveling along the road when suddenly a wheel broke. They brought a carpenter from a nearby village to fix it. The wagon started rolling along when suddenly one of the horses fell in his tracks and died. And so the guards had to buy another horse. This animal was hitched to the black van. The driver flicked his whip over its back and the animal began straining forward. But the van refused to move! The guards got off and tried to push the van, thinking that it had gotten stuck in some pothole in the road but no, the road was smooth and still the van would not budge! By now they realized that they could not fight against the Rebbe's strong will. They asked him if they could at least travel to a town and stay over in an inn. But the Rebbe saw that it was too late. They would not make it in time for *Shabbos*.

"Will we have to spend the next twenty-five hours in the middle of the road, out in the open?" they asked him. He said that they could go to a meadow and camp out there, off the road. As soon as he gave his permission, the horse suddenly leaped forward, as if suddenly released from his invisible bonds. The van was taken off the road and they settled down for the night and day, until *Shabbos* was over.

The Rebbe remained in jail until the ninteenth of *Kislev*, a date which is still celebrated today by Lubavitcher chasidim all over the globe as the Celebration of Redemption.

Striving for the Best

וַאֲשֶׁר הוּא עֹשֶׂה ה' מַצְלִיחַ

And all that he did, Hashem blessed with success (39:23)

R eb Gedalya Halperin of Skoli was a very prosperous man. Reb Gedalya had a government franchise for a cigar and cigarette factory in the town of Viniki. Government inspectors had to approve the tobacco which he bought and processed. But Gedalya did not only buy the government-approved tobacco. He also smuggled some tobacco of inferior quality into the factory and bribed the inspectors to overlook the corner where the poor tobacco was stored. This system worked for a long time, making a rich man of Reb Gedalya.

Once, a new set of inspectors sent from the capital descended upon the factory in a surprise check-up. They did their job thoroughly and discovered the poorer brand of tobacco. They duly made their report. Reb Gedalya would have to stand trial.

Before the actual blow fell, Reb Gedalya quickly traveled to his Rebbe, R' Meir of Premislan.

By the time he arrived in Premislan it was already late Friday afternoon, too late to see the Rebbe. He decided to let the matter wait until after *Shabbos*. Meanwhile, he tried to forget his worries and absorb the holy atmosphere at the Rebbe's court.

They were reading *Parashas Vayeshev* that week. As usual, the Rebbe read from the Torah. The Rebbe indicated that he wanted Reb Gedalya to be honored with the *shishi aliyah*. Reb Gedalya recited the appropriate blessings and the Rebbe began reading from the scroll. He read until he reached the words, '...and he (Yosef) was in prison.' even though the usual stop was three verses below. He indicated that Reb Gedalya was to say the closing blessing.

Reb Gedalya understood that it referred to him, that he was destined to go to jail. He paled and began trembling violenty. He had not told the Rebbe anything yet. Still, the Rebbe had indicated that he was fated to go to jail. How frightening! Reb Gedalya looked inside the Torah and suddenly realized that the reading was not really over. There were still three verses to *shishi* according to tradition. He certainly did not want the Rebbe to stop the reading at so unfavorable a place. His eyes pleaded with R' Meir to continue on until the usual *shevi'i* stopping point. The Rebbe obliged and concluded with the words, '...and all that he (Yosef) did *Hashem* blessed with success.' That was more like it! Reb Gedalya heaved a sigh of relief. That was a hopeful note to end on!

Shabbos passed uneventfully. After *havdalah* Reb Gedalya entered the Rebbe's study. He wished to pour out his troubled heart.

R' Meir, in his divine intuition, had guessed at the trouble. He said, "That was very clever of you, Reb

Gedalya, to make me continue on until *shevi'i*. But tell me the truth, don't you think that you deserve your punishment? You have been cheating the public all along! You have been producing an inferior product!"

Reb Gedalya hung his head in shame. Yes, he had realized that, already, on the way, and had been truly remorseful. R' Meir looked deep into his heart and saw that his regret was genuine. And he said, "I see that you are sincere. Very well, may I extend my blessing that you be spared all suffering, on the condition that you mend your ways in the future!"

When Reb Gedalya returned home to Skoli he learned that all charges against him had been dropped! There would not be a trial!

Prayer for Forgetfulness!

וְלֹא זָכַר שַׂר הַמַּשְׁקִים... יוֹסֵף וַיִּשְׁכָּחֵהוּ

And the butler did not remember... Yosef and he forgot him
(40:23)

Fortunate is the man who places his trust in Hashem...
and does not turn to the proud — this is Yosef
(Midrash)

R' Yisrael of Chortkov used to tell the following tale about his grandfather, R' Aharon of Titov, a grandson of the Baal Shem Tov:

As a young man R' Aharon lived in Konstantin. His

star had not yet begun to shine upon the horizon and no one knew who the poor young scholar behind the stove really was. He spent his days in study. No one seemed to care whether he had enough to eat or to feed his family because he never spoke to anyone.

When he could no longer bear the poverty in his home, R' Aharon stood up and movingly exclaimed aloud in front of all the people in the *beis medrash*:

"How long, will I have to be in your midst before you realize that I am the grandson of the Baal Shem Tov and that I am starving? Does no one ask or care?" "

The people were shocked by this revelation. No, they had paid no attention to the young scholar. Well, this must be remedied right away. The *gabbaim* met together at once and decided to allocate a weekly amount to R' Aharon.

Later, when the *beis medrash* had emptied out, R' Aharon burst into tears of self-reproach. "Why did I have to say anything?! Why did I have to ask for help? Have I not always managed until now, trusting upon *Hashem's* mercy and goodness? What a foolish thing I did, to become dependent upon the graces of mankind!" He wept bitterly. What could he do? Could he take back words that had already been said? No, he could not do that. But he could pray that *Hashem* would make the people forget that they had heard them!

All night R' Aharon prayed. He stood by the *mezuzah*, imploring *Hashem* to make the people forget what he had said.

The next morning he was at his usual place, behind the stove. No one took any notice of him; no one even stopped to say 'good morning'. He was hidden from sight. As for the commotion of the previous day when everyone had pledged to help him — that was all forgotten. His prayer had truly been accepted!

"It was from my grandfather," said R' Yisrael, "that I learned the simple explanation of the *Midrash* which states that Yosef was fortunate in not having put his trust in mankind. But the Torah specifically states that he asked the butler to remember him to Pharaoh! True, for one moment Yosef forgot to trust in *Hashem* and appealed to the butler. But he realized his sin at once and prayed to *Hashem* to make the butler forget the request. That is the meaning of '...and the butler did not remember Yosef.' Why? Because "he forgot him' — that is, Yosef made him forget him by praying to *Hashem* to erase the request from his mind."

Misplaced Trust

וְלֹא זָכַר שַׂר הַמַּשְׁקִים אֶת יוֹסֵף וַיִּשְׁכָּחֵהוּ

And the butler did not remember... Yosef and he forgot him
(40:23)

Because Yosef relied upon his remembering him — he was required to remain imprisoned for another two years
(Rashi)

R eb Moshe Chaim Rottenberg carefully opened the letter which the poor man had given him, with deep awe. He could see that it came from the famous Kotzker

Rebbe, R' Menachem Mendel. Reb Moshe Chaim read it through. The Rebbe was asking him to give generously towards the wedding expenses of this poor man's daughter. He went to a drawer and pulled out a single ruble, handing this to the poor man.

"What?! Is this all? I was led to expect that you would give generously. You are a rich man! You are also a respected man, the brother of the Gerrer Rebbe, the *Chidushei Harim!*"

The poor man begged and pleaded, but Reb Moshe Chaim would give no more. Deeply disappointed, he left. The poor man trudged along the road, wallowing in self-pity. Full of bitter thoughts, he walked along when suddenly he heard voices calling out to him,

"Wait! Wait up! Reb Yid, stop a minute!"

He turned around. It was the servant who had opened the door for him in Reb Moshe Chaim's house. He ran up to him with a heavy sack in his hand. "Here," the man said, thrusting the sack into his hand, "my master told me to give this to you."

The poor man opened the sack. There was enough money in it to cover all of his expenses! Was this a mistake? It made no sense, considering the rich man's previous behavior. Consumed by curiosity, he decided to retrace his footsteps and ask for an explanation. When he entered Reb Moshe Chaim's office, he asked him why he had given him only one single coin at first but then sent a huge sum by way of his servant.

The rich man replied, "When you entered here with the Rebbe's letter, you pinned all of your hopes on that piece of paper as the key to your salvation. Thanks to that letter, you felt confident that the money was as good as in your pocket already. You forgot that *Hashem* is the ultimate Provider and the only One in whom you should place your trust. I wished to bring you back to your senses and so I gave you one single coin. I forced you to think things over and realize that only *Hashem* — and not the Rebbe's letter — could help you. Only then did I send you the entire sum that you needed."

The Forgotten Letter

כִּי לֹא יַעֲשֶׂה ה' אֱ־לֹהִים דָּבָר כִּי אִם גָּלָה סוֹדוֹ אֶל עֲבָדָיו

For Hashem will not do a thing without first revealing His council to His servants

(Haftorah Parashas Vayeshev, Amos 3)

The Baal Shem Tov was not in his *beis medrash* in Mezibuz. He needed money for *pidyon shevuyim*. There were Jews languishing unjustly in jails and he must ransom them. And so the Baal Shem Tov and his close circle of disciples were off on a journey to raise a considerable sum towards this vital cause.

Along the way they stopped at an inn not often visited much by travelers, since it was off the beaten track. The Baal Shem Tov and his companions entered the inn, certain of a kind welcome. The innkeeper, a pious and wealthy Jew, outdid himself in his hospitality for it was not every day that he saw a Jewish face. And when he learned that his visitor was none other than the Baal

Shem Tov he was besides himself with joy. He hustled and bustled and fussed around his guests to make sure that they were comfortable and happy. Such a visit was cause for a feast! He slaughtered a calf and served up a lavish banquet for his guests. During the meal he learned the cause of the trip and gave a most generous sum for the *pidyon shevuyim*.

The Baal Shem Tov was very appreciative of all that his host had done. He thanked him and asked several times if there was anything that he could do for him. Did he have children? Were they in good health? Was his business thriving? The rich innkeeper insisted that, thank G-d, he had everything he could possibly desire.

"In that case, I would like to ask a small favor," said the Baal Shem Tov.

"A favor? Ask me anything at all, Rebbe. You have no idea how happy I am that you graced my humble home with your visit. I would do anything you asked! Try me!"

"It is really something insignificant and should not inconvenience you too much. Still, it is important to me. First I would like a pen and paper. I wish to write a letter."

The innkeeper ran to fetch paper and pen. The Baal Shem Tov wrote a few words, folded the sheet, then inserted it into an envelope. He sealed it and wrote two names and addresses upon the front.

"I want you to deliver this letter by hand. Do not send it by mail or by messenger. It is addressed to the *parnasim* of the Brodi community."

"It will be my greatest pleasure, Rebbe," he said, thrusting the envelope into his pocket.

The innkeeper rushed into the stable to harness the horses for the Baal Shem Tov. He leaned over a large wooden chest to pick up the leather harness straps when suddenly the letter slipped out of his pocket and fell into the chest without his realizing it. The innkeeper busied himself and now the Baal Shem Tov's coach was ready. The group climbed in and they were soon on their way. The innkeeper rode alongside for a short distance in his own cart and then turned back. The letter was completely forgotten.

Days passed, turning into months, months turned into years. The innkeeper paid occasional visits to Mezibuz but even this did not prod his memory. The letter was erased from his mind. Nor did the Baal Shem Tov himself mention it.

More time elapsed. The Baal Shem Tov passed away. Troubles began for the innkeeper. His landlord demanded a much higher rent. At first, the innkeeper struggled to pay, but when business fell off for one reason or another, he did not earn enough to cover the higher sum. After selling some of his household furnishings to meet one payment, he finally decided to leave. Sadly, he gathered up all of his belongings and prepared to move away. It was a very difficult decision. Had the Rebbe been alive, he would have gone to ask his advice, to get his blessing. But now he had no one to whom he could pour out his aching heart.

He went from room to room, gathering whatever was worth taking along to his new home. Not much remained of value; most things had already been sold. He started at the attic and made his way through the house until he came to the stable. Here he found several chests which had been used for storage. They would be excellent to keep his things in while he traveled around, looking for a new home. He dragged the chests outside into the sunlight. Something old and yellow caught his eye. He bent over and fished it out. It was a letter, addressed to two men in Brodi. The handwriting was familiar... This was the letter that the Baal Shem Tov had given him to deliver! It all came back to him in a rush.

The innkeeper suddenly felt weak. He had not delivered the letter! He had promised the Baal Shem Tov, assuring him many times that it was no bother at all... and then he had promptly forgotten all about it! Who knew what terrible damage he had caused by not delivering it? The holy Baal Shem Tov had depended upon him and he had failed him. He sat there, weeping bitterly. Looking all around at what had once been his, he wondered if all of his troubles had not resulted from his forgetting to deliver the letter! How could he have forgotten such an important thing! How many years ago had it been? Seventeen? Were the people still alive?!

The innkeeper stood up. He had made up his mind. He was going to Brodi, even if he had to go by foot! He bade his family 'good-bye' and began trudging down the road towards Brodi.

He walked steadily for many days. By the time he reached his destination he was thoroughly exhausted. His shoes were worn through, his clothes ragged, his appearance unkempt. He had lost much weight. His bones ached; his heart ached. What now? What if the men had passed away?

He made his way to the central synagogue of Brodi and sank down on a bench. He did not know anyone here. After he had rested for a few minutes, he walked over to the *shammash* and showed him the envelope.

"Do you know these two people? Do they still live in Brodi?"

The *shammash* shook his head. No, these names were not familiar but perhaps one of the worshippers could help him. The innkeeper went from person to person, asking the same question. People shook their heads or shrugged their shoulders. Finally he went to the older people. They might remember people from fifteen years back and know what had happened to them.

They looked at the names on the envelope. "To the *parnasim* of Brodi: so-and-so, so-and-so..." They shook their heads. "Brodi is a big city but to our recollection no such people ever served as *parnasim*. The office is usually held for several terms so we should remember. There must be some mistake."

"There cannot be any mistake! This letter was written by the Baal Shem Tov's holy hand! How could he have erred? It is inconceivable!" The innkeeper began arguing with the old men when suddenly two young boys rushed breathlessly into the synagogue.

"The election results have been announced. Brodi has two new *parnasim* out of the twelve! They are..."

The names the boys mentioned were the very ones written on the envelope! Everyone gaped in amazement. The innkeeper left without a word; he rushed out to find these two men. When he finally located them, he handed over the seventeen-year-old letter, his hands trembling.

They took it, opened up the age-stained envelope, withdrew a crackling sheet of paper and read:

"To the two new *parnasim* of the city of Brodi: The bearer of this letter is an innkeeper who has fallen on hard times. He is a worthy man who lived all his life in luxury but did not neglect to give generously and support every worthy cause. Do whatever you can to set him back on his feet and make him self-respecting once again.

I, Yisrael ben Sarah Baal Shem Tov, request of you to do your utmost."

This story was told over by R' Avraham Yehoshua Heshel of Apta, the *Ohev Yisrael*. In conclusion, he said:

"You are probably overwhelmed by the Baal Shem Tov's far-sightedness, by the vision with which he saw into a future beyond his own death. That is a truly remarkable feat but that is not what amazes me. I marvel at the great *tzaddik*'s love for his fellow man! The fervent *ahavas Yisrael* burned so deeply in his heart that he looked into this man's future to see if he could do anything for him. At the time of his visit, the innkeeper had had everything he desired. But in his gratitude, the Baal Shem Tov wished to help him in the future, when he would need it, when the Baal Shem Tov himself would not be there to help him."

פָּרָשַׁת מִקֵּץ

Parashas Mikeitz

Into the Burning Oven

וּלְהָשִׁיב כַּסְפֵּיהֶם אִישׁ אֶל שַׂקּוֹ

And to return each man's money to his sack (42:25)

Mar Ukva, one of the great Sages of Israel, had a poor neighbor to whom he gave four *zuzim* each day. Knowing that his neighbor might feel embarrassed, he would put the four *zuzim* in his satchel and as soon as he reached the poor man's house, would approach stealthily, lest anyone hear him, and quickly throw the money through a slot in the door. Then he would run away.

The poor man would find the money and have no idea of who gave it to him. Thus, he would not be embarrassed to keep it.

One time Mar Ukva stayed in the *beis midrash* longer than usual. He did not notice how time had passed, so engrossed was he in his study. But his wife became concerned, for it was very late. She finally went to the *beis midrash* to see if anything had happened to him.

When Mar Ukva looked up and saw his wife, he

stopped learning and got up to follow her home. He intended to drop the money off at the poor man's house, as he always did.

On this particular day his neighbor had decided to hide and discover who gave him the money. He kept watch by the window to see who was passing by.

Suddenly, he saw Mar Ukva and his wife walking along the street and turning down the path to his hut!

"These must be the kind people who are helping me!" he thought. He got up to go to the door, for he wished to thank them.

When Mar Ukva and his wife saw the door opening they ran. They did not want him to catch them and be embarrassed. They sought a place to hide. They found a huge oven belonging to a bakery. They ran in and closed the door behind them. The oven floor was still burning hot for the oven had been in use that day. Mar Ukva's feet were burned but his wife's feet were not. *Hashem* caused this miracle to happen; He wished to show the difference in the forms of charity. Mar Ukva's wife gave food to the poor. They were able to eat it right away, in her house, and appease their hunger. Mar Ukva, however, gave money and the poor had to go out and buy food and prepare it before they could quiet their hunger.

Mar Ukva and his wife had chosen to run into a fiery oven rather than embarrass a poor Jew!

Waiting for His Brother

הַבֹּקֶר אוֹר וְהָאֲנָשִׁים שֻׁלְּחוּ

Morning dawned and the men were sent off (44:3)

*To teach us that a person should always enter a city while
it is still light and leave a city after the sun has risen.*
(Tractate Pesachim 2a and Rashi)

During the Roman rule of *Eretz Yisrael* there was a
certain inn in the south of the country. Its owner
was an evil man though he was clever in hiding his
wickedness and no one suspected him of being anything
but honest. Many people, indeed, came to stay at his
hotel.

In the middle of the night, the innkeeper would wake
up his guests to get them started on their way.

"Get up!" he would shake them. "It is time to get up!"

They would look at him in surprise but seeing him all
dressed to go, would also get up. Their 'kind' host would
offer to accompany them and show them the road since it
was dark and he was traveling anyway.

The hotel guests would have no choice. They would get
dressed and start on their way, accompanied by their
host.

Little did the people realize that behind his innocent
appearance lurked a wicked man. The innkeeper was in
partnership with a band of robbers. They knew
beforehand when he would be leading his guests along
the road. They would attack, tie up their victims, steal
everything they had, and then finally free them. The

innkeeper would share in the loot with his partners.

No one suspected anything for a long time. No one dreamed that the innkeeper could have a hand in such dreadful crimes.

One time, however, R' Meir happened to visit this inn. He ate supper and went to bed.

It was still dark when he felt someone shaking him, urging him to rise. He rubbed his eyes and saw the innkeeper, all ready for travel.

"It's time to get up and be on your way. I have to travel, too, and will accompany you to show you the way."

R' Meir had no desire to get up right then and became very suspicious. Why was the innkeeper so insistent? Why was he so eager to leave while it was still very dark? R' Meir remembered that the Torah also warned people from the dangers of night. It urged travelers to find safe lodgings while it was still daylight and not to leave before the sun had risen. And so he replied, "I cannot go yet. I am waiting for my brother. When he comes, we will travel together."

"And where is your brother?" he asked in honeyed tones. "Let me fetch him so that you will not be detained because of him."

"My brother is in the *beis haknesses*," R' Meir replied.

"In the *beis haknesses*? And what is his name?"

"His name is Ki Tov."

The innkeeper left his inn, full of high spirits, and went to fetch Ki Tov from the nearby synagogue. He reached the threshold of the building and called inside, "Ki Tov! Ki Tov! Hurry up! Your brother is waiting for you!"

But no Ki Tov appeared.

Disappointed and angry, he returned to his inn. Dawn had broken already and the sun was shining by the time he reached the inn. R' Meir, who had already completed his morning prayers, was all set to continue on his way. This time, the wily innkeeper had not succeeded in his wicked scheme. Angrily, he turned to R' Meir and asked, "And where is that brother you were waiting for? Why are you leaving without him?"

A broad smile flashed on R' Meir's face. "Oh, my brother has already come," he explained. "Don't you see that the sun has already risen and that it is day? Regarding the light, our Torah says: 'And *Hashem* saw the light that it was good.' The *light* is my brother Ki Tov!"

(According to *Midrash Rabba Bereishis* 92:6)

How is it Possible to Steal?!

וְאֵיךְ נִגְנֹב מִבֵּית אֲדֹנֶיךָ כֶּסֶף

And how could we steal money from your master's house?
(44:8)

When the *Sfas Emes*, the Gerrer Rebbe, first visited the Kotzker Rebbe, he was shocked. The house was wide open. No one locked doors; the silver was kept in full view, in unlocked cabinets. Anyone could come in and walk off with anything!

"Everything is *hefker* here, wide open! Is this a way to run a home?!" he asked.

He complained to the *shammash*, Reb Feivel, and the *shammash*, in turn, went to the Rebbetzin. "What do you expect? Why shouldn't things be stolen if the house is open to everyone, if no one keeps an eye on anything?"

When the Kotzker Rebbe heard, his voice rang out,

"Feivel! How can anyone steal?! Does the Torah not state 'Thou shalt not steal'?!"

When the *Sfas Emes* told this over later to his own chasidim, he added, "When I heard the Kotzker Rebbe's thundering voice I was overwhelmed. It seemed to me as if stealing was altogether impossible, inconceivable! How could anyone take something that did not belong to him — the Torah explicitly stated that stealing was forbidden!"

My Life for His

נִכְמְרוּ רַחֲמֶיהָ עַל בְּנָה

Her pity welled up for her son
(Haftorah Parashas Miketz, Melachim I, 3)

It was the custom in Berditchov, that just before *Yom Kippur* people came with their *kvittlach*, notes, and two coins, asking the Rebbe, R' Levi Yitzchak, to pray for them on the holiest of all days.

Who in Berditchov did not want a good year? Who did not want the great *tzaddik* to pray for him?! Everyone came with their notes. Everyone found the money to put on the Rebbe's table.

One particular *erev Yom Kippur* the Rebbe sat by his table for hour after hour. The pile of notes heaped up on one side, the heap of coins piled up on the other. And still the Rebbe waited. What was he waiting for? There were so many preparations to make for *Yom Kippur*!

Shortly before *Kol Nidre*, a woman rushed in; she put her note on the table and next to it — two coins.

The Rebbe studied the note, then looked at the two coins. "There are two names here but you only brought two coins. You must either give me two more coins or delete one of the names," he said firmly.

The woman heaved a deep sigh and explained, "I am a widow. All I have in the world is my dear son. Our two names are those in the note. But what could I do? I rushed about all day long trying to scrape together these two coins. I begged and borrowed but still could not get more than this. What shall I do, Rebbe?" she was on the verge of tears.

"My rule is firm. I cannot make any exceptions for anyone. You must decide yourself — who do you want me to pray for: you or your son?"

She sighed but did not hesitate. "For my son, of course! He is my most important treasure. I would sacrifice my life for his!" The woman had made her decision. The Rebbe nodded and she left.

As soon as the words were out of her mouth, the Rebbe rose and went joyfully to the synagogue where the people were already waiting for him to begin *Kol Nidre*. And as he walked along the streets of Berditchov he muttered over and over,

"I am going to pray for my people, the Jewish people, upon the merit of this poor widow. She is willing to sacrifice her life for the sake of her son, *Ribono shel olam*! So must You, *Hashem*, have mercy upon Your sons, Your chosen people."

With these words the Berditchover strode confidently towards the *amud* and began the *Yom Kippur* prayers.

פָּרָשַׁת וַיִּגַּשׁ

Parashas Vayigash

Among the Poor

אֲנִי יוֹסֵף אֲחִיכֶם אֲשֶׁר מְכַרְתֶּם אֹתִי מִצְרָיְמָה

I am Yosef your brother whom you sold to Egypt (45:4)

Even in my office as viceroy I have remained the same humble, lowly person whom you sold down to Egypt.
(Beer Mayim Chaim)

R'Akiva once went to the market to sell a precious pearl. Along the way he met a poor, unfortunate person dressed in rags who always sat in the *beis knessess* amongst the poor.

How surprised R' Akiva was when that poor man approached him, gazed at the precious stone and said, "I want to buy that!" When he noticed R' Akiva's astonished look, he added, "Come along home with me. I will pay for the stone when we get there."

R' Akiva was certain that the man was playing a joke on him. How could such a ragged person have the means to buy such a precious gem?

Nevertheless, he followed him. His house was a huge mansion. When they approached it, the servants came out to greet their master. They carried out a golden chair, placed him upon it and began washing his feet.

The ragged man said to them, "Give R' Akiva the price he is asking for his gem, then set a table for us."

R' Akiva now understood that the man was not poor at all. On the contrary, he was very wealthy indeed!

After they had eaten, R' Akiva turned to his host and asked, "Why do you degrade yourself, going around in rags and sitting among the poor?"

The man replied, "R' Akiva, it says: 'Man is compared to vapor; his days are like a passing shadow.' I am well aware that money has no lasting power and cannot accompany a person after death. Thus I realize that keeping company with the downtrodden and the miserable is good for me. It prevents me from boasting about the wealth which *Hashem* has granted me. That way I feel akin to everyone, equal to all men. For do we not all have one Father; did not one G-d create each of us? Is it not better for me to sit among the poor than to be boastful, sin and end up in *gehennom*? *Hashem* despises the haughty."

R' Akiva's eyes lit up at this explanation and he left the magnificent home after praising and blessing his host.

(According to the *Midrash* noted in *Menoras Hamaor* 332)

The Shammash's Condition

אַל תֵּעָצְבוּ וְאַל יִחַר בְּעֵינֵיכֶם כִּי מְכַרְתֶּם אוֹתִי הֵנָּה

Do not be grieved and do not be distressed that you sold me here (45:5)

The Rebbe's reception room was full. People were waiting for hours for an audience with the *Chidushei Harim*, R' Yitzchak Meir Alter of Ger.

Reb Bunim, the devoted *shammash*, a man of kind nature, kept watch and saw that each one was received in proper order.

But one chasid rushed forward, demanding to enter before his turn. Reb Bunim asked him to sit down and wait patiently, but the man insisted that he had to go in. He had an urgent request. Everyone's request was important, the *shammash* pointed out. Everyone had to wait his turn. The man jumped up and slapped the *shammash* across the cheek. Reb Bunim was overwhelmed. He immediately went in to tell the Rebbe what had happened without naming the guilty party.

Everyone in the waiting room was shocked. No one spoke a word. They each sat quietly, awaiting their turn. Reb Bunim ushered them in, one by one, to pour their troubles out before the Rebbe. The man who had slapped Reb Bunim also went in, but the Rebbe sensed that he had given the slap. He refused to speak to him until Reb Bunim would accept his apology.

"But Rebbe,' he wept. "I am a broken man. I have come here to ask you to pray for me that I be blessed with a child. My wife and I have been married for many years but we are all alone. Please listen to an unfortunate man's plea!"

"I will not listen to a word until you ask Reb Bunim to forgive you. You did a terrible thing. If he does not forgive you, I will bar you from here forever!"

The broken-hearted man went outside. He realized how shamefully he had behaved and truly regretted his rash act. Going over to Reb Bunim, he humbly asked for his forgiveness. "I am a childless man," he explained, "and in my suffering I did not realize what I was doing."

Being kind by nature, Reb Bunim forgave him, seeing

that he was truly sincere. The man went back into the Rebbe's room but the *shammash* came in with him this time.

"Rebbe," the latter said, "I am willing to forgive him. But only one one condition."

"Yes? What is your condition?" the Rebbe asked.

"I will forgive him only if the Rebbe agrees to bless him with children!" Reb Bunim said.

The Rebbe smiled. His *shammash* had driven a good bargain. The *Chidushei Harim* did bless the man and within a year he became a proud and happy father.

How to Punish

אַל תֵּעָצְבוּ... כִּי מְכַרְתֶּם אוֹתִי הֵנָּה כִּי לְמִחְיָה שְׁלָחַנִי

Do not be grieved and do not be distressed that you sold me here (45:5)

It was a joyous occasion, a wedding at which many prominent rabbis were present, among them the *Admorim* of Trisk and of Husyatin. During the wedding a young man somehow insulted the Rebbe of Trisk. The Rebbe was willing to overlook the matter but when the Rebbe of Husyatin learned of it, he said,

"We cannot let this go by! I demand that the young man be brought to a *din Torah*! R' Yaakov Weidenfeld, the noted author of 'Kochav MiYaakov' should judge this case."

However, the Rebbe of Husyatin saw that the Rebbe from Trisk was not at all pleased with the turn of events.

And so, looking at the young man, who stood trembling, he held up his hand and said,

"Just one minute. Let me tell you a story before you do anything hasty. There was once a similar case of a young man behaving disrespectfully to the *parnasim* of Ostrow. He was summoned to a *din Torah* before R' Yaivi. This is how R' Yaivi settled the matter: Turning to the trustees, he said: 'You realize that this young man is poor. He has no means. If I were to fine him, he would be unable to pay up. Find some task for him, some way to serve the community. Thus he will learn the value of communal responsibility and will gain a new respect for you too!'

"Here, too," the Rebbe of Husyatin concluded, "this young man who insulted the Rebbe of Trisk is penniless. How can we fine him? I suggest that instead, the Rebbe of Trisk bless him with prosperity. Then, when the blessing is realized, the young man will surely appreciate his greatness and will feel all the more remorse for having been disrespectful to him!"

The End of the Third Day

אַל תִּרְגְּזוּ בַּדָּרֶךְ

Do not quarrel along the way (45:24)
Do not get involved in a halachah discussion, lest the road
become unsteady (you lose your way)

(Rashi)

When R' Yisrael of Salant learned Torah, he did it with great intensity. He expended extreme amounts of energy in concentration, so much so, that his body began to suffer. Once, he reached such a state of physical exhaustion that his doctors forbade him to study for three whole days.

R' Yisrael was very careful to obey doctors' orders and now he also heeded the doctor's warning even though it was very difficult for him. The next three days were very, very long. Towards the end of the third day, at sunset, his family saw R' Yisrael standing outside, looking intently at the sky to see if any stars had come out as yet.

When he noticed the attention he was generating, he explained, "A sick person is freed from the responsibility of keeping many *mitzvos*. He is an *onus*, under coercion. Then he has only one obligation — to watch over his health! By getting better, he will be able to perform all of the *mitzvos*. It is then that his evil inclination, concentrates all of his efforts against that single *mitzvah*. He tries to persuade the patient, through all kinds of deceptively righteous excuses to avoid this obligation to get better as soon as possible!"

Dance — and Be Saved!

וַתְּחִי רוּחַ יַעֲקֹב

And the spirit of Yaakov was revived (45:27)

Yom Kippur in the Baal Shem Tov's court was over. The *shofar* had been blown to signal the end of this holy day. All prepared, as in every Jewish congregation, to begin the year right away with a *mitzvah*, with the blessing of the new moon. They rushed out but to their dismay, the moon was obscured by thick grey clouds. The chasidim went back in to the *beis medrash* to wait for the clouds to disperse. They were disappointed, but their sense of well-being after *Yom Kippur* bubbled up inside them until it rose to the surface. A circle of chasidim formed in the hallway and began dancing. It grew and grew until it spilled over into the Baal Shem Tov's study.

No one noticed how sad the Baal Shem Tov looked. He felt that something had been missing in his *Yom Kippur*. Was this the reason that the moon was hiding its face? How could he begin the year, the new account of good deeds, without the immediate *mitzvah* of *Kiddush levanah*? Looking out of the window at the clouds, which showed no signs of dispersing, the Baal Shem Tov grew sadder and sadder. He shut his eyes tightly in concentration and began praying.

But the chasidim were oblivious to the Rebbe's mood. In their enthusiasm they pulled the Rebbe into the circle. He could not resist them and joined them, somewhat reluctantly, until he, too, became uplifted by their wholehearted joy.

The room rang with the happy sounds. Then suddenly someone exclaimed, "Look! The moon is out! The moon is out!" The room emptied as everyone rushed out to perform the first *mitzvah* of the year.

With a look of happy astonishment on his face, the Rebbe exclaimed, "What I had hoped to accomplish with my prayer — and failed — you, chasidim, have accomplished through your joy!"

R' David Moshe of Chortkov told the following story:

"A chasid once came to me to pour out his woes. He

was soon to stand trial for a very serious offense. His chances of being acquitted were very slim — he might even have to pay with his life! Full of fear, pain and bitterness, he wanted solace from me.

At that very moment, the chasidim were dancing joyously in the large entrance of the *beis medrash*. I turned to this poor chasid and told him the story of the Baal Shem Tov and the *kiddush levanah*. I told him that a person must put his implicit trust in *Hashem* and serve Him always with joy. Even at the worst of times, in his greatest tribulations, a man must be secure in his faith that *Hashem* will save him — and rejoice in this reassurance. *Hashem's* salvation will come to him from out of that joy!

And now — I said — go and join the dancing circle. Rejoice and you will be saved!

That chasid went out to dance. He soon forgot his woes and in truth, in the end everything turned out for the best!"

The Bed of Sorrow

וַתְּחִי רוּחַ יַעֲקֹב

And the spirit of Yaakov was revived (45:27)

The Shechinah rested upon him because of his joy.
(Rashi and Chazal)

It was a strange situation. There were dozens of excellent carpenters in Ostila. R' Yossele had visited each and every one of them, but when they heard what he wanted, they all turned him down. All R' Yossele wanted was a new bed, a bed for the Chozeh of Lublin who would soon be coming to visit him.

Knowing R' Yossele, one might ask why he needed a new bed when his house was very well furnished. This certainly was not the first time that someone would be staying in his home. Was the Chozeh so particular that no bed was soft or comfortable enough for him?

It was very unusual, but whenever the Chozeh slept on a bed which had not been made especially for him, he suffered terribly. He felt needles pricking his flesh. He would groan and moan with real pain even though there was not a single needle, not even the slightest splinter that might disturb his sleep. There was something very significant about his suffering, something very deep — and puzzling.

R' Yossele had gone from one carpenter to another, expecting each one to feel privileged to make a new bed for the *tzaddik*. But everyone had refused him...

All except one poor carpenter. This craftsman was not poor because his work was inferior. Whatever left his workshop was a masterpiece. But he did not work much, preferring to spend most of the day in prayer and study. He only worked to cover his expenses.

It was this carpenter that R' Yossele visited last. Hopefully, he stated his request: "I need a special bed made. The Chozeh of Lublin is to sleep on it. You must go to the *mikvah* before you start work on the bed and while you are making it, you must think only pure thoughts."

To his great surprise, the carpenter agreed. He spent many days purifying himself. During those days he would pray fervently that his labor find favor, that it be blessed with success. And when he worked on the bed, his thoughts were constantly on holy matters.

Finally it was completed. R' Yossele was overjoyed at the finished product and had it carefully transported to his home. Here he covered the bed with a new mattress, with snowy-white linen, comfortable pillows and a light featherbed. Next to the bed he put a table with washbasin and towel, a chair and a lamp. Then R' Yossele carefully locked the door and hid the single key where only he had access to it. G-d forbid, that anyone touch that bed now!

All that was left now was to wait for the Chozeh's arrival. R' Yossele was on pins and needles.

The Chozeh finally arrived in Ostila. R' Yossele was the first to rush forward to greet him.

"Rebbe!" he exclaimed, trembling with emotion, "Would you do me the great honor of staying with me while you remain in our city? I have prepared a special room and have even had a new bed made for the Rebbe! It was made by a very pious and deserving carpenter."

To his great joy the Chozeh agreed! R' Yossele took his revered guest home and led him to his room. He unlocked the door and begged him to rest for a while from his difficult journey.

Confident that the bed would meet his approval, R' Yossele left the room so that his honored guest could rest. To his great dismay, he soon heard moaning and groaning coming from the guest room.

"Oy! Vey! It hurts! Needles are piercing my bones!" Before long the *tzaddik* was actually weeping from the intense pain.

Who can describe R' Yossele's consternation and alarm at the sound of those terrible cries? How could it be? After all the precautions he had taken! Was the *tzaddik's* soul so sensitive that even this special bed was not worthy of giving him rest? R' Yossele did not know what to do.

He could not bear to hear the Chozeh's distress. Knocking discreetly at the door, he asked if the Chozeh wanted to rest on his own bed, perhaps. The Chozeh agreed.

He sank down on R' Yossele's bed but did not utter a word. R' Yossele tiptoed out of the room, hardly daring to breathe. He stood outside a few minutes but still did not hear a sound.

The Chozeh slept for some time. When he got up he thanked his host gratefully. "Now I truly feel refreshed. You have poured new life into my weary bones!"

R' Yossele was very glad. But he was puzzled as well. Gathering his courage, he asked, "Perhaps you can explain to me why the bed which was made by a most worthy Jew, especially for you, a bed that was never even slept in, was not suitable while my own bed enabled you to sleep most comfortably?"

The Chozeh explained, "The bed which was made for me was truly made with intense *kedushah*. Through and through. But it was made during the Three Weeks of Mourning over the *Beis Hamikdash*. The craftsman who made it was so steeped in sorrow over the destruction and over the exile of our people, that it penetrated every inch of the bed. It is a bed of sorrow, weeping and compassion. How could I not feel it? And how could such emotion allow me rest and sleep?"

The Power of Good News

וַתְּחִי רוּחַ יַעֲקֹב אֲבִיהֶם

And the spirit of Yaakov, their father, was then revived (45:27)

The Ziditchover Rebbe's grandson lay ill. Everyone was praying for him, all the sons and grandsons of the Rebbe. Nevertheless his condition grew worse from day to day. R' Sender Lipa, the Rebbe's first-born and the child's father, was distraught.

The situation grew so critical that late one night the doctor feared that the end was near.

The Rebbe was accustomed to devote the late hours to holy study and prayer. No one ever disturbed the Rebbe when he secluded himself in his attic room, shutting the entire world out of his consciousness to concentrate on his sublime thoughts. But if the Rebbe was not told now — it might be too late...

The Rebbe's sons — the sick boy's uncles — thought and thought. Whom could they send to disturb the Rebbe without incurring his wrath? They finally decided to send Yehudah Tzvi, who later grew up to be the famous Doliner Rebbe, the Rebbe's favorite grandson.

With a small lantern in his hand, the lad climbed up the narrow staircase leading to the attic where his grandfather secluded himself. When he reached the door, he hesitated and then coughed.

The Rebbe heard, rose and went to open the door. "Nu?" he asked.

Little Yehudah Tzvi beamed up at his saintly grandfather, his cherubic face aglow. "I have come to tell you good news, Zeide! Your grandson is feeling better! But you still must pray for his complete recovery!"

The Rebbe beamed with joy and motioned to the boy to enter his study. He then went over to a cupboard and took out some herbs. He put them in a small paper bag and handed it to the boy. "Tell your aunt to boil this up into a tea and give it to the patient while it is still hot. It will make him sweat and he will get better!"

The little boy thanked him and rushed out of the room, down the stairs and straight to his uncle, R' Sender Lipa, with his instructions. The tea was made and given to the patient, spoon by spoon. Within hours he had passed the crisis and recovered completely!

The next morning R' Sender Lipa went to his father to tell him that his son had recovered.

The *tzaddik* looked sternly at his son and said, "You can learn a lesson in chasidus from your nephew, Yehudah Tzvi! You, with your long face and worried looks, only increased my own anxiety and suffering. But that little boy knew exactly what to do to change my mood to a happy one. And once my spirits were lifted I felt divine intuition returning to me and I knew at once what to do to bring about the patient's recovery!"

Following Yaakov's Example

וַיֶּאְסֹר יוֹסֵף מֶרְכַּבְתּוֹ וַיַּעַל לִקְרַאת יִשְׂרָאֵל אָבִיו

And Yosef harnessed his carriage and went up to greet his father Yisrael (46:29)

He, himself, harnessed the horses to the carriage in his eagerness to honor his father.

(Rashi)

R' David of Lelov, who lived in Jerusalem, sent his son abroad. He knew that it was for his son's own good that he spend a few years in Poland studying Torah. Still, those years dragged on endlessly for the doting father.

Finally, the time came for the son to return to his father. Both awaited the reunion with aching, yearning hearts. The entire city rejoiced with the Rebbe over the imminent return of the young man.

Then one day he was finally there! He reached Jerusalem towards evening and rushed to his father's *beis medrash*. The Rebbe did not give his son more than one fleeting glance, then turned to the *baal tefillah* and nodded that he begin the *maariv* prayers.

It was only when the prayers were over that the father finally turned to his beloved son with a warm *shalom aleichem* and enveloped him in a loving embrace.

The chasidim who were present understood exactly what the Lelover Rebbe had done: he had followed the example of Yaakov Avinu. Yaakov, when he met with his beloved Yosef whom he had not seen for twenty-two years and whom he had thought to be dead, did not fall upon his son's neck but, says the Midrash, recited the *Shema*. Yaakov wished to capture the love which welled up in him when he saw his son and dedicate it wholly to *Hashem*. He wished to show that his love for *Hashem* was even greater than that for his beloved son, to bear out the verse of the *Shema* — "And you shall love *Hashem* your G-d with all your heart..."

R' David of Lelov wished to follow this very same example.

Honoring One's Parents

וַיֵּבְךְּ עַל צַוָּארָיו

And he wept on his neck 46:29)

But Yaakov did not fall upon Yosef's neck and did not kiss him for he was reciting the Shema.

(Rashi)

"**A**vimi, my son, truly fulfills the commandment of honoring one's parents!" said the *amora* Abahu about his son, R' Avimi.

The people present asked, "How does R' Avimi fulfill the *mitzvah*?"

R' Abahu related the following: "My son Avimi has five sons, all rabbis and scholars. They all still live at home. Whenever I come to visit, it is my own son, Avimi, who comes to answer my knock at the door. He could ask any of his own sons to do so but prefers to keep that *mitzvah* for himself."

He continued, "And while he is rushing through the corridor, he keeps on reassuring me loudly, 'I am coming! I am coming!' He wants even my waiting to be pleasant and not impatient!"

R' Abahu once asked his son Avimi to bring him a glass of water. The latter rushed to fulfill his father's request. Even so, when he arrived with the glass he saw that his father had already dozed off.

He stood there, bent over his father all the time, waiting for him to awake. His hand was outstretched all the while, waiting for the moment when he could immediately fulfill his father's request!

(According to Tractate *Kiddushin 31*)

A Speedy Peace-making

וְעָשִׂיתִי אֹתָם לְגוֹי אֶחָד בָּאָרֶץ

And I will make them into one nation in the land
(Haftorah Parashas Vayigash, Yechezkel 37)

There was a fierce controversy raging in a Jewish community. The entire town was split down the middle. One half would not speak to the other half or if it did, it was only with harsh words and angry shouts. People from neighboring villages heard about it and were deeply concerned. What a terrible state of affairs! They rushed to R' David of Lelov, begging him to arrange a peace settlement between the two fighting factions.

R' David took along his closest disciple, R' Yitzchak of Vorki, and traveled to the town. They reached it just in time for *davening*. Without even stopping to talk to anyone, they began praying along with the rest of the congregation. When they had finished praying, R' David ordered the coach and they traveled back.

R' Yitzchak was very puzzled and asked, "Rebbe, we did not even do anything. Why didn't you stay to speak to the people? What have we accomplished? Why are we returning already?"

The Rebbe allayed his fears. "Don't worry. By uttering the words in the *shemoneh esrei* prayer 'Oseh shalom bimromav... — He Who makes peace in His heavens, He shall make peace amongst us and over all of Israel' — I already accomplished everything that there was to do in this city!"

The Most Suitable Day

וְכָרַתִּי לָהֶם בְּרִית שָׁלוֹם... וְנָתַתִּי אֶת מִקְדָּשִׁי בְּתוֹכָם

And I will make a peace covenant with them... And I will put My sanctuary in their midst
(Haftorah Parashas Vayigash, Yechezkel 37)

The eminent R' Refael of Bershid, one of the great chasidic leaders, specialized in marriage counseling. He was an expert in making peace between troubled couples.

Once he visited a strife-ridden couple and tried to restore love and peace between them. He chose an unusual time for this; it was *Tishah B'Av*!

When he was later asked why he had not postponed this visit to another day, he replied,

"The *Beis Hamikdash* was destroyed over baseless hatred, *sinas chinam*. Jews could not get along with one another. What better day to try to make peace between a man and wife than on *Tishah B'Av*!"

פָּרָשַׁת וַיְחִי

Parashas Vayechi

The Table Was to Blame

שִׂכֵּל אֶת יָדָיו כִּי מְנַשֶּׁה הַבְּכוֹר

He crossed his hands, for Menashe was the firstborn (48:14)

Since Menashe was the firstborn, he did not want him to be embarrassed in being placed to his left and therefore crossed his hands

(Commentaries)

It was the first night of *Pesach*. In Posen, R' Akiva Eiger was seated by his table, celebrating the *seder* together with a table full of guests. The table was spread with a snowy white linen tablecloth, the best the family had. Beautiful silver and crystal dishes gleamed after hours of polishing in preparation for this special night. Everyone was about to lift his wine goblet for one of the four required *kossos* when suddenly one of the guests overturned his goblet. The rich purple wine sloshed all over the beautiful tablecloth.

Stealthily, R' Akiva Eiger began to shake the table until his own goblet also spilled.

"Oh my!" he cried out. "This table must be shaky!" He thus spared his guest from embarrassment.

The Fox Who Had a Cold

בִּקְהָלָם אַל תֵּחַד כְּבֹדִי

In their assemblies shall my honor not be joined (49:6)

My name should not be mentioned in connection with dissension

(Midrash)

A raging controversy had developed between two different groups of chasidim. The followers of R' Meir'l of Dzikov were very concerned and wished to investigate the matter in the hope of making peace. The Rebbe, however, dissuaded them from becoming involved.

"Let me tell you a story," he said.

"It was a year of famine. The animals of the forest had grown lean. They had a continually hungry look in their eyes. But the king of the forest, the lion, suffered most of all. One day, after not having eaten for three days, he felt very weak; a foul odor arose from his mouth. If he did not find prey soon, he was afraid that he would die! Letting out a mighty roar, the lion summoned his servants. The horse was the first to rush to his side.

"'Draw near and tell me what you smell,' said the lion. The horse bowed his head towards the lion's mouth and said, 'There is a foul smell coming from your mouth, Your Majesty!'

"'You traitor! How dare you insult the king! You shall die for your arrogance!' And with these words, he

pounced upon the horse and made a hearty meal out of him.

"His hunger was satisfied for a while but after a few days the lion again felt his stomach grumbling for food. His hunger grew so intense that a bad odor again arose from his mouth. He gave a mighty roar, summoning his servants, the beasts of the forest. This time the wolf answered his call.

"'Draw close to me and tell me what you smell,' the king ordered.

"The wolf did not wish to make the same mistake as the horse. He said, 'I do not smell a thing, Your Majesty!'

"'Liar!' the lion shouted. 'You are a traitor. You deserve to be killed!' With one mighty leap, he fell upon the wolf and made a hearty meal of him too. A few days passed and again the lion was assailed by pangs of hunger. Again his mouth reeked from fasting. He gave a piercing roar, summoning his servants, the beasts of the forest, to him. This time the fox came first.

"'Yes, Your Bajesty, what cad I do for you?'

"'Draw near and smell my breath. Tell me, what do you smell?'

"The fox began coughing and sniffling. He said, 'Your Bajesty, I cad't sbell adythig today. I have a terrible stuffed dose. I caught a dasty cold...'"

The chasidim smiled as the Rebbe brought the message home, saying, "You must behave like the clever fox and not stick your noses into any dangerous fires of controversy. You will only be hurt..."

For What Purpose Wisdom?

וַיַּרְא מְנֻחָה כִּי טוֹב וְאֶת הָאָרֶץ כִּי נָעֵמָה וַיֵּט שִׁכְמוֹ לִסְבֹּל

And he saw repose that it was good and the land that it was pleasant, and he bent his shoulder to bear (49:15)

To bear — the yoke of Torah

(Rashi)

Eliyahu Hanavi told the following story: I was once walking along a road when I met a person who ridiculed me and made fun at my expense. I asked him, "What will you have to say on the Day of Judgment when they ask you why you did not study Torah?" He replied: "I have the perfect excuse: I will say that heaven did not grant me wisdom, intelligence and sense to understand Torah."

"And what do you do for a living?" I asked. He replied: "I hunt birds and catch fish."

"And who gave you the intelligence to know how to take flax and weave it into nets for your snares? And after you have caught the fowl, how do you know how to market them?"

The man replied, "Heaven blessed me with the sense to know that."

I then challenged him: "If you have the intelligence to hunt birds and catch fish, surely you have enough intelligence to study Torah too!"

The man thought about what I had said and suddenly began crying. And from that day on he devoted himself to the study of the holy Torah.

(According to *Seder Eliyahu Zuta, Chapter 14*)

Not Recognized

וַיֵּט שִׁכְמוֹ לִסְבֹּל

And he bent his shoulder to bear (49:15)

To bear — the yoke of Torah

(Rashi)

R'Eliezer ben Charsom inherited a great estate from his father and was very rich. He owned entire cities and a large fleet of ships. He employed hundreds of workers and servants in all of his undertakings and establishments.

However, he himself did not take any interest in the actual running of his business and ventures; his employees never even saw him. R' Eliezer devoted his days and nights to learning Torah.

Each day he would take a pitcher of flour and place it on his shoulder and go thus to the *beis midrash*.

One day while on his way to learn, some of his servants stopped him. They thought him to be one of the inhabitants of R' Eliezer's towns and demanded that he pay the road toll since he was using the road that R' Eliezer had built!

They barred his way and would not let him go without paying. When he refused, they forced him to come along with them and work off his debt.

R' Eliezer, who was a humble person, did not tell them who he was. He asked, "Please allow me to continue on my way to the *yeshivah* so that I can study Torah!"

They would not let him go. They swore and said, "By

the life of R' Eliezer ben Charsom, we will not release you!"

R' Eliezer saw that they were determined to make him work. He gave them a large sum of money so that they allow him to go on his way to study Torah!

(According to Tractate Yoma 35)

Where Are the Musicians?

וַיֵּט שִׁכְמוֹ לִסְבֹּל

And he bent his shoulder to bear (49:15)

To bear — the yoke of Torah

(Rashi)

R' Chaim of Volozhin had not seen his brother, R' Zalman, for a long time. But now that he was celebrating the marriage of his son, his saintly brother, R' Zalman, had come. R' Chaim was overjoyed. He wanted his brother's stay to be a joyous and memorable one. "I will send the musicians over" he said. "They will put you in excellent spirits and liven you up."

R' Zalman nodded in thanks and went to his room to wait for the musicians. He sat in a chair and — never one to be idle — began reviewing a certain difficult passage in *gemarah* by heart. He was soon so deeply engrossed in his study that he did not even notice the door open. Three musicians entered: a drummer, clarinet player and a violinist. They saw R' Zalman sitting in a chair, waiting. They arranged their instruments and began playing, at first softly.

R' Zalman nodded, his lips moving. They took this as a sign of appreciation and began playing louder, with a rhythmic beat and a lively tempo. The room reverberated to their music. Their enthusiasm grew, the more they played, especially since it seemed to them that their respected audience was so appreciative that he was singing along! After they had played a few numbers with all the energy they had, they bowed and left the room.

R' Zalman sat in his chair, just as before. Some time later his brother, R' Chaim, came in.

R' Zalman looked up at him and asked, "Nu, where are the musicians you promised to send to me?"

The Power of a Pipe

וַיֵּט שִׁכְמוֹ לִסְבֹּל

And he bent his shoulder to bear (49:15)

To bear — the yoke of Torah

(Rashi)

S moking is a difficult habit to stop, once started. But great men are able to do so once their mind is made up. This is the story of how R' Shalom of Belz cured himself of the habit:

R' Shalom enjoyed a good pipe of tobacco. He would puff away even while studying in the *beis medrash*. Perhaps he thought it helped him to concentrate. Anyway, it put him in a good mood. He smoked his pipe, day in and day out, until one day he gave up smoking.

While looking up from his *gemarah*, he noticed one of the regular worshippers of the *beis medrash* preparing his pipe for smoking. He saw the man cleaning out the pipe carefully, knocking out all of the old ashes, twisting a pipe cleaner in between all the crevices and making sure that it was thoroughly clean. He then took out his tobacco pouch and began filling it with tobacco. This took quite some time. He filled it, pressed down the tobacco, filled it again, pressed it down again until it felt heavy enough in his hand. Then he had to get it lit. This also took time. He puffed and puffed but still the tobacco did not catch fire before the match burned out.

R' Shalom took this all in. Then he returned to his study, forgetting all about the pipe-smoker. When he had finished the entire *blatt*, the page of *gemarah*, he happened to look up. He noticed the smoker taking his first real puff after having successfully lit the ready pipe.

The man had been working over his pipe for the whole time that it took him to study an entire page of *gemarah*! What a disgraceful waste of precious time! R' Shalom took out his own pipe, held it at arms length and said with utter disdain, "If this object has the power to cause so much *bittul Torah*, such outright waste of time — I will have nothing to do with it any more. From now on it will not enter *my* mouth!"

And that is how the Belzer Rebbe stopped smoking!

A Tzaddik Decrees

What a terrible disappointment! R' Bunim had traveled all the way from Pshischa to Strikov — only to find that the Rebbe was receiving no one; no one was to be admitted, the family said. Those were R' Fishele's very strict orders.

"Why? What has happened to make the Rebbe behave thus?" R' Bunim asked.

The Rebbe's closer followers sighed sadly, and explained to R' Bunim what had happened. "The Rebbe has lost confidence in his powers. Not long ago, a poor man came weeping to him. He had tried his hand at many things but was successful in none. Now that his money was all gone, he begged the Rebbe to advise and bless him. The Rebbe told him to go out and buy a lottery ticket and he did so at once. When the drawing was made, the man saw that he had not won anything! Terribly disappointed, he went to the Rebbe. He had taken the Rebbe's advice and had lost everything. The Rebbe took it very much to heart. If Heaven denied him the power to help people, then there certainly was no further point in listening to their woes! And since that bitter day the Rebbe has refused to admit anyone. That is the situation. Now you understand."

R' Bunim listened to this tale but was not disheartened.

"I don't care. I will enter the Rebbe's study at my own risk for I hope to make him change his mind and see things in a different light."

Without even waiting for their consent, R' Bunim turned the doorknob and entered the room. At first R' Fishele's eyes lit up at the sight of his visitor but then he became downcast again. He could not help R' Bunim, no matter how much he wished to do so.

R' Bunim sat down opposite the Rebbe and began speaking, "The power of a *tzaddik* is a very puzzling thing. Our Sages said that 'a *tzaddik* decrees and *Hashem* guarantees.' On the other hand, in our prayers we ourselves admit that 'who, of all Your creations, in the heavens above or the earth below, can tell You what to do...?' This seems to be an out and out contradiction! How are we to understand both concepts? Does *Hashem* carry out the wishes of the *tzaddikim* or does He do as He pleases? The truth is a combination of both. *Hashem* does take into consideration what a righteous man asks of Him. But He does not like to be dictated to. *Hashem* does not have to be told *how* to carry out the *tzaddik*'s decree, for He has many different messengers, many different ways of helping the person for whom the righteous man prays. Only *Hashem* decides which way to help the downtrodden and the afflicted."

I am certain," continued R' Bunim with confidence, "that the Jew whom you prayed for will eventually be helped. For R' Fishele's prayer is not expressed in vain. But who is to dictate to *Hashem* that the man be helped precisely by a lottery ticket and not by some other way? Since you have decreed, though, that man will surely be helped."

These words were like balm for the troubled R' Fishele.

He agreed to open his doors once again to those in trouble and to pray for them. R' Bunim's prediction was not long in being fulfilled. The poor Jew who had not won with his lottery ticket was indeed helped through some other miraculous way and lifted out of his poverty. The tzaddik's decree was fulfilled after all!

The Minister and the Priest

וְעַתָּה שָׂא נָא לְפֶשַׁע עַבְדֵי אֱ-לֹהֵי אָבִיךָ

And now, forgive the sin of the servants of your father's G-d
(50:17)

The virulent power of evil gossip! What hatred *lashon hara* can sow in people's heart! It was only the venom of malicious talk that caused bad relations between R' Tzvi, the *Admor* of Stertin and R' Meir of Premislan.

A young man, an ardent follower of both great men, was greatly distressed over the controversy that raged between the two great men and resolved to do something about restoring good feelings between R' Meir and R' Tzvi. When his wife gave birth to a boy, the chasid invited both *Admorim* to come to the *bris*, one as *mohel* and the other as *sandak*, without telling either that the other was invited.

Early on the morning of the *bris*, the father hired a fine

coach and went to fetch R' Tzvi, the *mohel*. On the way
home, he said that he had to stop off and pick up the
sandak as well. He drove to R' Meir's home in Premislan
and got out of the coach to fetch him. When he returned
with R' Meir, R' Tzvi, turned his face away, refusing to
greet or even look at him. R' Meir, known for his
generous, forgiving heart, was not insulted. Instead, he
said:

"Let me tell you a true story: This happened during the
Spanish Inquisition when Jews were forced to either leave
the country or give up their religion. Many of them, the
Marranos, renounced their religion but remained Jews in
secret.

"One time a government minister lay on his deathbed.
A 'converted' Jew, he knew that if he did not summon a
priest to hear his dying confession and to give him the
last rites, he would be endangering his entire family. He
allowed a priest to be summoned but when the priest
arrived, he pretended to be too weak to talk. The priest
asked the doctor if the patient was really so weak. 'No,'
the doctor replied. 'He is dying, but he is not too feeble
to accept the last rites.' When the priest saw that the
minister had turned his face to the wall, he guessed that
he really did not want to die as a Christian. The priest,
who was a Marrano himself, ordered everyone to leave
the room, since he must hear the confidential confession
of the dying man. When everyone had left the room, he
bent over the patient and whispered the *shema* in his ear.
With a smile of relief, the minister turned his face to the
priest and together they said the Jewish *viduy*, before his
soul departed. "

R' Meir finished his tale and thrust out his hand in a
friendly gesture to R' Tzvi. "*Shalom aleichem, R' Tzvi!*" he

said. "Are we not both Jews, both serving one G-d? We have a common goal in life. Why should we not strive towards it together?"

R' Tzvi smiled, taking R' Meir's hand in his own. And peace reigned between the two once more.

Accepting Abuse

וְאַתֶּם חֲשַׁבְתֶּם עָלַי רָעָה אֱ-לֹהִים חֲשָׁבָהּ לְטוֹבָה

You intended evil against me but Hashem reckoned it for good
(50:20)

A great Rebbe once heard a man being abused and embarrassed. His face showed how deeply hurt he was. Hoping to appease him, the Rebbe went over to him and said comfortingly,

"Did you know that, when heaven passes a harsh decree against a person, *Hashem* sometimes sends it to him in the form of abuse? Although this is very painful and hurts deeply, still, in the long run, it is much easier to bear than actual punishment. This is how you must regard your disgrace now.

"You must learn to accept all humiliation and mortification with actual joy, not only resignation. You must understand each time that by accepting this as a form of punishment, you are sparing yourself greater suffering. You must never bear a grudge or plan revenge.

By being humble and holding oneself to be no more than dust, a person can spare himself harsh decrees and even death. Humility and acceptance can actually increase a person's life span! Let me tell you a story that illustrates this very aptly:

"It happened in the time of Napoleon, the great world conqueror. The French emperor swept through many countries. No one offered any resistance to his mighty forces. He penetrated deep into Russia before he finally came up against a certain fortified city which withstood his fire. The walls held firm against the French barrage. Napoleon stubbornly decided to lay siege and wait until the city fell from starvation and thirst.

"The French soldiers camped all around the city, not allowing anyone to enter or leave. But the city showed no signs of weakening. Napoleon's forces, on the other hand, itched for battle. They could not bear the idle waiting. If they could not fight, they wished to return home.

"Some of his officers came to the emperor to report the soldiers' restlessness. It was a dangerous sign, they warned. Napoleon was in a quandary. His pride would not let him leave the city unharmed. He needed to learn if they were on the verge of surrender, or if they still had plentiful stores of food and ammunition. He decided to disguise himself as a peasant and together with another disguised officer, slip into the city and spy out the situation. Only then, could he decide whether to continue the siege or retreat.

"It was the middle of the night when he and the other officer made their way into the city, dressed as Russian peasants. With no one suspecting them, they headed straight for a tavern.

"That particular tavern happened to be a favorite meeting place of Russian soldiers. They would gather there and drink themselves into a stupor, forgetting their troubles. Drawing near, the two Frenchmen had no trouble listening in on the conversation. They learned that the situation was indeed critical. The city was starving. 'Do you know what?' one soldier confided. 'At headquarters they are already talking about surrendering to Napoleon! We hardly have a chance!'

"Napoleon and his companion tried hard to hide their joy. And then it happened! One of the soldiers looked directly at the spy and said, 'Hey! Look at this peasant, will you? Doesn't he look exactly like Napoleon? I am ready to swear that it is he! No mistake!'

"'Don't be a fool!' his officer hastened to reply. 'Do you think that Napoleon himself would stoop to spying? Do you think that the French emperor would risk his life in such a dangerous mission? Don't be a fool! Only an idiot would enter the lion's den.'

"Just to show his soldiers, the officer turned to the Russian peasant and ordered him to bring a glass of beer. Napoleon got off his chair, went over to the bar and asked the bartender for a glass of beer. Just as he was about to put it on the table in front of the officer, he purposely dropped it. The glass crashed to the floor, spraying beer in all directions. At that moment his companion, the French officer, got up and began screaming at his awkwardness. He kicked him to the ground and when Napoleon managed to get to his feet, slapped him across the face, cursing his stupidity.

"The Russian soldiers guffawed hilariously. Turning to their companion, they said, 'And you thought that this fool was Napoleon!'

"'Ha, ha, ha!' laughed another soldier. 'Who would have dared treat Napoleon like that! You must be crazy to have even imagined it!'

"Meanwhile the French officer went over to settle his bill, including the damage of the broken glass. Then the two left the tavern, having accomplished their mission. They slipped through the city streets and managed to return to the French camp outside the city.

"As soon as they were on safe ground, the officer fell to the emperor's feet and wept, 'Please, Your Majesty, forgive me for striking you. Surely you realize that I only dared do so because it was the only way to save your life, to make sure that no one dreamed that you were the real Napoleon!'

"Napoleon drew him to his feet and embraced him heartily. He chuckled and said, 'If I knew that by returning your blows I would be doing you a like favor, I would certainly do so. However, I will reward you painlessly, pleasantly, for the blows and abuse that you gave me which saved my life. I will promote you to a position of honor and reward you with many precious gifts!'

"It was not long before the city walls were finally penetrated. Napoleon's forces entered and with hardly any effort succeeded in capturing the city.

"Now you understand, dear friend, how valuable even blows and abuses can be..." concluded the Rebbe.

The Camel's Solution

וְהַעֲלִיתֶם אֶת עַצְמֹתַי מִזֶּה

And you shall bring my bones from here (50:25)

The Rambam had never been happy living in Egypt, the accursed land which had enslaved his people. And so, just before he was about to die, he gathered his family and close friends together and, like Yosef, made them promise that they would bring his remains to *Eretz Yisrael* to be buried.

After having been assured that they would do so, the Rambam was able to breathe more freely. A few days later he died and his soul rose up to the heavenly vaults. All of Egypt mourned, not only the Jews. Everyone had held this great man in high esteem. But the Jews felt the loss very deeply. For one full week they mourned. When the week was over, a special casket was ordered of fine, strong wood. The Rambam was placed in it and the coffin was loaded upon the back of a camel.

Jews all over the world mourned the Rambam's passing. And in *Eretz Yisrael*, they went to meet the coffin. When the funeral procession arrived, the *Eretz Yisrael* Jews asked the Egyptian Jews where the Rambam was to be buried.

"He did not specify," they replied. "The Rambam did not state any preference. Therefore we leave that matter entirely up to you."

Jews in the different cities all over *Eretz Yisrael* wanted the holy man to be buried in their city. What an honor it would be to have the Rambam's grave nearby! The

Jerusalemites made claim to the privilege, arguing that their city was the gateway to heaven, the site of the *Beis Hamikdash* and now, of its remnant, the Western Wall. It was only fitting that such a great man join the other holy leaders buried on *Har Hazeisim*. The residents of Hebron claimed that such a great man must be buried next to the Patriarchs: Avraham, Yitzchak and Yaakov and their wives, the *Imahos*, who were buried in the *Mearas Hamachpela*. No place else was good enough! The Jews of Meron wanted the Rambam buried next to R' Shimon bar Yochai, author of the sacred *Zohar*. Each settlement had a good reason why it should have that great privilege.

And so the controversy raged, every group pulling in a different direction. All of *Eretz Yisrael* was torn by dissension.

Meanwhile the funeral procession had stopped. It did not know which direction to take. The camel stood by patiently, bearing its holy burden. But this was a disgraceful situation! The body must be buried as soon as possible; the burial had already been postponed so long. In the end, the people unanimously decided to let the camel take the initiative. The beast would be allowed to go wherever it wished; it would lead the way and make the critical decision where the *tzaddik* was to be buried.

The camel began walking. It walked and walked with its head held high, neck arched, looking almost regal. The entire procession followed behind. And as it walked, many people joined the funeral march, striding behind the camel bearing its holy load. It walked northward, people noticed, until it finally reached the city of Tiberias. Here it crouched down to rest.

The Rambam was buried on that very spot. And his tomb is there to this very day!

The Ten Partners

וְלִבְנֵי בַרְזִלַּי הַגִּלְעָדִי תַּעֲשֶׂה חֶסֶד... כִּי כֵן קָרְבוּ אֵלַי

And to the sons of Barzilai the Giladi shall you show
kindness because they came close to me
(Haftorah Parashas Veyechi, Melachim I, 1)

There once lived a wealthy man who was blessed with everything a person could possibly wish for. Money, prestige, property, sheep, cattle and most precious of all — ten stalwart sons, his pride and joy. He lived in ease and comfort, lacking nothing to make him happy.

There was one thing, however, that disturbed his inner peace. He was afraid that after he died his sons would fight over the inheritance. Would his wealth be a curse instead of a blessing? Or would the brothers continue to live together in peace and happiness as they did now, in his lifetime?

As he grew older, this worry gave him no rest. One day he called his ten sons together and said: "My dear sons. You know that I am concerned for your future. I want you all to be happy. But I cannot help dreading that when I die you will begin quarreling over the inheritance and will no longer live as brothers. You will be beset by jealousy and hatred."

The sons hastened to reassure their father that such a terrible thing would never happen! They would continue to live in peace even after he left them. The father was happy to hear this, but still did not wholly rely upon their promises.

"I know that your intentions are pure. I am grateful for that. But I also know that you are only human. A person cannot always rule over his desires or jealousies. I have decided to divide up my money in my lifetime. I will give each one of you a decent share so that you can set yourselves up. I will set aside one thousand *dinar* in ready cash. Each of you will receive one hundred *dinar*. This is a considerable sum. Invested wisely, it can grow and grow and make you each rich. As for the rest of my assets: my house, fields, orchards and cattle — that you can divide after I die."

The sons wept to hear their father talking about death but promised to stay together and live as brothers.

Time passed and the man's fortune turned for the worst. A heavy drought wrought havoc upon his fields, vineyards and cattle. Soon he was forced to sell everything to pay off his debts. The only thing he would not touch were the thousand *dinar* that he had promised his sons. But times grew so hard that he finally had to dip into this sum. He took fifty *dinar* from the thousand, much as it pained him. This hurt him so much that he actually became ill and before long, lay on his deathbed. He now summoned his ten sons and began dividing up the remainder of the money.

He began with the firstborn, giving him his full hundred. The second and third sons also received the full amount he had promised and so on, down the line. When he came to the youngest, he began weeping. "What can I do, my dear son? Hard times have come upon us. When I first promised you one hundred *dinar* in my lifetime, I never dreamed that I would have to dip into the money to pay off my debts. I had hoped to leave you all fertile fields, lush vineyards, fat cattle. But now I cannot even give you what I promised! I gave your brothers one hundred *dinar* each. Now I only have fifty left. But even these are not all yours. I still have to deduct some for expenses; all I can spare for you are twenty *dinar*. Take them and forgive me, my son. I know you will, for you have the kindest heart of all your brothers."

The youngest son was disappointed at having received such a small sum but was even sadder that his father was so grieved. "Father!" he cried, "Do not be troubled! It doesn't matter. I forgive you!"

Suddenly he was hit by the realization of how paltry a sum he had actually received. "But all I have is twenty *dinar*. What will I be able to do with it? It is not enough for any serious investment!"

"Don't worry, my dear son," the father reasssured him. "Listen to my advice. I have ten faithful friends. I am sure that they will help you in your time of need. Believe me, loyal friends are worth more than money, worth even more than one thousand *dinar*!"

A few days later the father returned his soul to his Maker. The ten sons mourned his passing and after the week of *shivah*, each went his own way.

There was nothing left to divide after the father's death. Each of the nine sons were eager to make the best of their one hundred *dinar* and did not even stop to think about the youngest brother. Each invested the money as best he could and soon became totally involved in his own business affairs.

What could the youngest do with his twenty *dinar*? There was not enough money to do anything worthwhile. Before long, it was all used up in daily expenses. Only one single *dinar* remained.

The son looked dolefully at the single coin. Suddenly

his father's words of advice sprang to his mind. The ten loyal friends! He had inherited his father's good friends! This was a valuable asset, his father had assured him. But what was he to do? To ask them for money? To beg?! Certainly not. Besides, that was not a lasting solution.

He sat down and thought things carefully over. Finally he came to a decision: "Come what may, I must honor my father's dying wishes. He wanted me to keep contact with his friends. That was his parting advice to me. I know! I will make a feast for them to gladden their hearts."

The youngest son went out to the market and with his last gold *dinar* bought meat and fish, rare fruits and tempting delicacies for a grand banquet. Then he invited his father's ten friends. They accepted, happy that their late friend's son was taking an interest in them. They wished to keep up the friendship with him too. On the appointed day they all came and feasted themselves upon the excellent meal. They ate and drank and were merry. It was a pleasant atmosphere, one of camaraderie and friendship. They reminisced about old times when their friend had been alive and they had often met at his home. They recalled how, in his prosperity, he had often helped them. Their thoughts turned to the other nine sons, their host's brothers, and someone commented, "Look, of all the ten brothers, only this son has remembered us! Only he has kept up contact with his father's friends."

Another joined in, "This feast must surely have cost him a large sum and I know that he does not have money to spare. His father did not leave him any inheritance for he had nothing to give him. How kind and thoughtful of our host to have invited us!"

"Let us repay him for his goodness!" a third suggested spontaneously. Everyone chimed in their fervent agreement. They agreed then and there to help out the youngest son, each man giving a cow which was about to give birth plus a money gift. Before the feast was over, they had sent their servants home to make good their promises.

All ten cows gave birth shortly, increasing the youngest son's possessions by another ten head of young cattle. The youngest son sold the calves and earned a large sum. From then on, everything that he did was blessed. Before long he was a very prosperous dairy and cattle farmer whose wealth exceeded that of his nine brothers.

Whenever he thought about his father's advice, the youngest son would sigh happily and say, "How right my father was! Indeed, friendship and loyalty is worth more than all the money in the world."

(According to the *Sefer Hamaasiyos* of Rav Nissim Gaon)

All Depends on the Letters

וְשָׁמַרְתָּ אֶת מִשְׁמֶרֶת ה'... לְמַעַן תַּשְׂכִּיל אֵת כָּל אֲשֶׁר תַּעֲשֶׂה

And you will guard the guardpost of Hashem... so that you
will be wise in all that you do

(Haftorah Parashas Vayechi, Melachim I, 2)

Two businessmen, both chasidim of R' Meir of Premislan, rented a forest from the local landowner. After they had signed a lease with the landowner, they came to R' Meir, asking him to draw up a partnership agreement between them, lest any argument ever arise. They wanted their partnership to be based on honesty and fairness so that it would be long-lasting.

But R' Meir demurred, "I am not a scribe," he said. "I cannot make up the complicated document that you want according to the exact *halachah*." He paused, then continued, "But I can write a brief agreement consisting of only four letters: *alef, beis, gimmel, daled*."

The two businessmen looked at him in bewilderment. What did he mean? R' Meir explained himself: "These are the four things which you must always keep in mind for they go hand in hand: *alef* — *emunah* or trust; *beis* — *brachah* or blessing; *gimmel* — *geneivah* or stealing (dishonesty) and *daled* — *dalus* or poverty."

They were no wiser despite his 'explanation' and still looked at him in puzzlement. R' Meir finally interpreted his strange words. He turned to them and said, "If you trust one another and remember the *alef* of *emunah*, then you will enjoy the *beis* of *brachah* in all of your endeavors. But if, G-d forbid, one of you steals or is dishonest, forgetting the *gimmel* of *geneivah*, then your partnership will suffer from *dalus*, poverty. This is the basic principal of any agreement."